Forever Temptation

A BE TEMPTED NOVEL

LOCKGROVE BAY
BOOK 3.5

CAZ MAY

First Published 2026
Paperback ISBN 978-0-6454683-7-3
Published by Caz May
© Caz May 2022-2025
Cover image from Shutterstock (VAndreas)
Cover editing by Caz May
Editing by Samantha Wolf

Love never gives up, never loses faith, is always hopeful, and endures through every circumstance.

— APOSTLE PAUL, 1 CORINTHIANS 13:7 (BIBLE)

Australian Slang Glossary

Ute-Truck
Bludger- someone lazy, doesn't do much and possibly relies on social security benefits
Ripper- something really good/great
Ridgy-Didge- Cool
Bonzer-Great, awesome
Pash/ing/ed-to kiss/make out
Arvo-afternoon
Chunder- Vomit, throw up
Gobby- Blowjob
Aussie Kiss- going down on a girl
Daks-pants/trousers/underwear
Undies/Knickers/Jocks-underwear (female knickers, male Jocks, undies both)
Dakking/ed- to pull or have pulled someone daks down (see above)

Bathers- universal name for female swimwear

Budgie Smugglers- small male swimmer that looks like underwear (google this one to see)

Thongs- Footwear, otherwise known as flip flops

Esky-Cooler-you keep drinks cool in it

Dunny-toilet

Bogan-white trash/trailer trash

Old Fella-Your father/Dad

Franger- Condom, Trojan etc

Milo-a malt chocolate powered drink mix (can be made hot or cold)

Macca's-MacDonalds

Fair Dinkum-used to emphasise or seek confirmation of the genuineness or truth of something

Fucking/Bloody oath- similar to above, but an extreme or emphasised way of saying yes.

Shark Week/Rags- A woman's monthly cycle

Stuffed if I know-a nicer way to say fucked if I know

AFL-Australian Rules Football

Fuck me dead.-oh my god, holy hell, struck dumb

Grouse- Describe something as great, terrific or good.

Giving me a view of her breakfast- showing your underwear from clothes to short.

PLAYLIST

FEATURED SONGS

FOREVER AND FOR ALWAYS-Shania Twain

I AM YOURS-NeedToBreathe

FULL PLAYLIST ON SPOTIFY

Preface

This story is set in my Lockgrove Bay world. There are multiple books out in this series which are currently published on Amazon.
Search Caz May or follow the below links to purchase.
This story is not a standalone story and will not make sense if you haven't read book 1 and book 2 of Lockgrove Bay at a minimum. Reading the rest of the Lockgrove Bay stories will only make your reading experience richer. This is Book 3.5 of the main Lockgrove Bay stories.

See links below for Book 1 and Book 2:
Bk 1- https://mybook.to/LoathingTemptation
Bk 2- https://mybook.to/WickedTemptation

See the below graphic for the full Lockgrove Bay reading order. Please don't hesitate to reach out if you have any questions about the books or the order of reading.

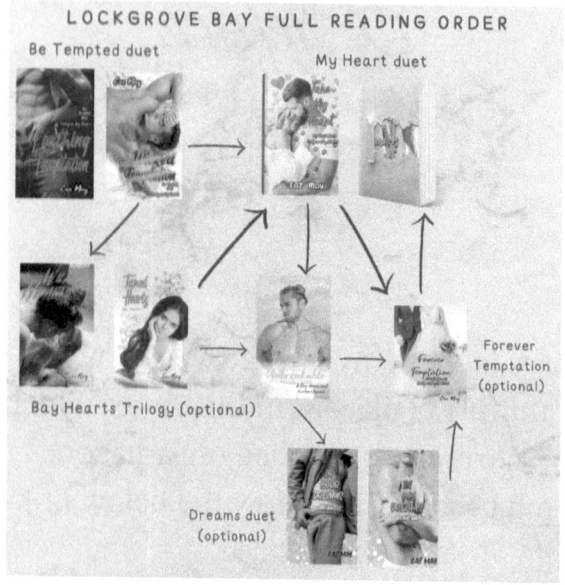

CHAPTER ONE

Ashton

I f you'd told me even a year ago, after graduating from Uni–me with a Bachelor of sports science with honours and Tempany with a Bachelor of Education–that we'd be back in Lockgrove Bay, I'd have laughed in your face. Like really fucking laughed, hard and with a sucker punch to the guts as well.

Five years ago, I wanted nothing more than to get away from Lockgrove Bay, but now–after some shit in the city–I couldn't be happier to be back in my quaint beachside hometown. It was like coming home, stupid cliches' and all. I wanted Melbourne to be home–and thought with Tem by my side that anywhere could be home, but there was always something missing.

It wasn't anything like not being happy with

1

Tem or missing a person in particular, but just a longing to be somewhere that had my heart. The only other people that weren't with me in the city were mum and my stepdad–Tempany's dad–Mathias. Ezekiel–my best mate and younger sister's boyfriend– lived with us. But once we all finished Uni, nothing was keeping us in the city. And rather than be jobless, living in a house that wasn't feeling like home we made the move back to Lockgrove Bay.

Having sold the townhouse we had enough cash to buy a couple of houses in Lockgrove Bay, one for Tem and me, and one for Zeke and Ava as well, even though I'm still wary of my best mate and sister being together. It's been years, and he's more than shown he loves my little sister, but old habits and memories make me edgy. I'd probably not be so cautious if he'd make a full commitment and put a damn ring on her finger, but I'm not going to rush him.

I'd proposed to Tem practically five years ago, and we'd decided to wait until we finished Uni. But we didn't count on feeling lost, and we sure as hell didn't think she'd have two miscarriages and be on the verge of a mental breakdown because of them. Seeing the woman I love in so much pain–physical *and* emotional–broke my heart. All I wanted to do was make it better, and she pushed me away, confiding in her best friend Lorena, even though she was in Lockgrove Bay with her husband Beau and their two kids. That was another pull towards moving back home–getting my fiancee' back closer to her best friend. I'd blocked out the pain of that time by getting shitfaced with Zeke, surprised that my carefree best mate actually gave a shit and let me cry on his shoulder.

God, look at me, being a cry baby. A twenty-three-year-old crybaby. It's not my fault that crossing the car park–after parking my mustang–I'm feeling memories and emotions hitting me hard, walking into the schoolyard.

It's my first day as the basketball coach, and Zeke's first day as a music teacher. Just the thought of my crass as hell best mate being a teacher makes me laugh so hard my sides hurt. I still remember the day Tempany came back to Lockgrove Bay–the first day of year twelve–and Zeke landed us in detention by taunting Mr. Daniels about his sex life during the holidays. He'd blatantly suggestively flirted with Miss Miller, our P.E teacher. And honestly, if Ezekiel wasn't so damn in love with my sister, I'd have thought he'd have gone after Miss Miller.

Speaking of, she's the first person I see as I open the door to the staff room. It feels odd–forbidden–to be entering this space.

"Well, well, fancy seeing you here, Ashton Castello," Miss Miller says with a wide smile, coming towards me and pulling me into a hug.

"Hi, Miss Miller, nice to see you," I reply, feeling as though I'm back in high school. It's a little weird to have her hugging me.

"Please, Ashton. Call me India now. I'm not your teacher anymore."

"Right, India it is," I reply, nodding when the door smacks open and the air in the room is charged with the exuberant presence of none other than Mr Ezekiel Alessio.

"Good morning, fuckers!" he bellows, crossing the room and eyeing India like she's his long lost lover. It rubs me the wrong way.

"Tosser," I greet him, turning his gaze off India to me. "You're with my sister, remember?"

"I know, Mr Castello," he taunts me. "Just seeing if Miss Miller here is still immune to my charm."

I scoff under my breath, and India laughs. "Hi, Ezekiel. Never thought I'd see you back in the halls of Lockgrove Bay either."

"It's good to be back, Miss M. Honestly," he says to her with a smile. "Is it still Miss?"

"Yeah, it is, but I'm getting married next weekend actually."

"Nice," Zeke replies, pulling her into a hug. He's sure being a weirdo.

"So, you're engaged or married to Ava Castello?" she asks him, and he blushes.

"We're together, yeah. Not engaged or married yet though," he confirms, elbowing me in the side.

"And you Ashton?" India asks.

"I'm engaged to Tempany Davies. Haven't set a date yet though."

"Oh my gosh, Ashton! That's amazing!" she shrieks excitedly. "Childhood *and* high school sweethearts." She's swooning, and it makes me smile.

"Yeah, we are. She's working over at the primary school, and got a class of grade one's."

"Oh, that's lovely. I'm so glad things have worked out," she replies when the first bell sounds through the halls.

"Yeah, it's good to be back in the bay," I tell her with a nod. "I'll probably catch you in the gym later. First thing for me is to organise tryouts for the team."

"No worries, have a great first day," she tells us, heading over to the kitchenette to grab a coffee.

Zeke again elbows me in the side. "Didn't think Miss Miller would still be a hottie," he says with a laugh.

"Yeah, but don't, Zeke. If you even think about cheating on Ava, I'll have your head on the wall as a trophy of *don't fuck with the new basketball coach*."

"Woah, Ashy, man, calm ya farm, bro," he starts, seeming nervous. "I'd never cheat on Ava. You know that."

"I know, I'm sorry. Just nervous for today."

"Me too, bro. But you'll kill it. Best coach Lockgrove Bay Prep has ever had, I know it."

He slaps me on the back when the second bell sounds. "Thanks for the confidence, man. Catch ya at recess."

"You bet, just like high school all over again," he says, laughing as we head out of the staff room into the corridors, now full of students rushing to class.

Pushing my shoulders back, I command the halls, heading into the sports storage ready for my first day as head basketball coach of the Lockgrove Lions. It's a dream come true, and I can't help the smile on my face. Coming back to Lockgrove Bay was definitely the right decision. It feels right–like home–and I'm ready for all that's about to be thrown at me, including the ball that hits me in the back of the head.

CHAPTER TWO
Tempany

I can't believe I'm here, in my very own class, as the teacher. The last few years have been a mix of heartbreak and joy. Having Ashton by my side as we graduated was amazing. But then losing two babies—only months apart—at seven and nine weeks completely broke me. Having Ashton definitely helped, but I'd wanted to share the news with my step mum and couldn't. It felt like I had no one to confide in, no one in my corner, and I missed home. The city would never feel like home without my dad and step mum there. It helped that Ava had come to live with us, but I missed the tranquility of Lockgrove Bay.

And being back I can't believe I'm here, on the very first day of living one of my dreams. The lunch bell rings, and after instructing my students to grab their hats I usher them out the door to the playground.

Quickly I slip on my orange hi-vis vest, grab my first aid bumbag, and follow my students out.

Walking around the playground on yard duty I'm feeling a mix of emotions. I love seeing all the students playing happily, shrieking with glee, but also I'm saddened that I might never get to see my own child playing with such happiness. I know that two losses doesn't mean we'll never have a child, but we'd been not preventing pregnancy for nearly two years, and Ashton and I had a lot of sex. He was so damn insatiable. But lately, things had dwindled with my emotions over the losses, and then moving back home, being together physically had been pushed aside. I do miss being with him.

I'm lost in thought, thinking naughty things about my fiancé when some older —grade six— girls come up to me, giggling excitedly.

"Are you Miss Davies?" One of them asks eagerly, her friends giggling and fidgeting as they look me up and down.

I smile at them and reply, "Yes girls, I am."

They giggle even more, and another says, "You're so lucky."

I laugh, wondering why they're so excited to know who I am. "Why?"

"Cause you're engaged to Ashton...well Mr. Castello, right?"

Right, there it is. These girls have a crush on my fiancé. "Yes, I am," I tell them, not able to hide my smile.

"He's so hot," they admit with the crazy giggles again.

I'm not sure what to reply. Yes, Ashton is hot, but I can't exactly say that to twelve-year-old girls.

"Ok girls," I reply, engaging my teacher's voice to say firmly, "run along and play ok."

"Ok," they say collectively, running off, smiling at me.

Coming back to Lockgrove Bay was definitely the right choice, but I think I need to talk to Ashton about our wedding because I'm afraid it's going to become bigger than the royal wedding. It seems like the whole town will want to be in attendance, that my fiancé is practically royalty in town. That's not far from the truth. I had to interview for my job, but Ashton basically got handed his job as coach of the high school basketball team on a silver platter.

The end of my playground duty is nearly over when an announcement blares over the speakers, "Miss Davies, could you please attend first aid."

I turn to my colleague who I exchange the vest

and bumbag with. She chuckles softly. "Must be one of your students with an injury."

"Most likely. First day dramas," I say heading inside to the first aid in the main office building.

The nurse smiles and laughs when she sees me.

"Oh Tempany, love, your class is being covered for the rest of the arvo."

She pauses and I give her an incredulous look. "Oh, why is that?"

"Your fiancé took a ball to the head earlier, and they called us to let you know. We thought you might like to help him home."

"Thank you, I'll grab my things and head over to the high school now."

I laugh as I head back to my classroom to grab my bag and keys. Definitely a crazy first day.

CHAPTER THREE

Ashton

Back home after another day as the basketball coach, I'm in the zone, reliving my teenage years with Zeke over, playing call of duty.

Zeke's character falls to his death at my shot, and he throws his controller down.

"How's things been this week, basketball coach?" he asks me as a distraction.

"Fine, Ezekiel," I taunt him, frantically pressing buttons on the controller.

"So no more balls to the head then?" he teases me, laughing.

"No, dickhead," I snap back.

"That's good, you've already lost enough brain cells."

"You're an arse, Ezekiel, and you've most

likely lost all your brain cells. I'm surprised you can even form words."

"Low, Ashton," he barks at me, his eyes on the screen as my character dies.

"Sorry, bro. I'm just teasing you. Never thought you'd become a teacher."

"Me either, but I'm enjoying it. I love seeing the students connecting with music," Zeke tells me.

"Yeah, same with basketball."

I glance across at my best mate, holding up the controller. "Another game or wanna switch to Fifa?"

"Fifa, bro," he replies, picking up his controller as I close out the call of duty game and get Fifa up. It starts loading, and I zone out a moment, shocked when Zeke asks, "Is Tem ok?"

His question is way off court, but I answer anyway, "Yeah. Why wouldn't she be?" I gulp, starting to scroll through the options to set up the Fifa game.

"Well, Av's noticed she was off the other day at Briston and Jeb's housewarming."

I give my best mate a glare, worried about what he's implying.

"What are you fucking on dipshit?"

"She was like giving Ariel glares, just like

you're giving me now...you know when she was with her kids."

I scoff, replying, "Well you know we want kids, dufus. It's just been so hard with the losses."

"I know man. But you should talk to Tem."

"I will," I reply, starting the game by kicking the ball around the on screen field.

"And Ash man?" Zeke says.

"Yeah?"

"I'm glad you've confided in me, but I really hate keeping secrets from Av's."

"I know, bro. But please don't let anything slip for me."

"I won't bro. I promise," he tells me, nodding towards the door when Tem strolls in, Chinese takeaway in hand.

"Thanks," I reply, just as Tem kisses me as I stand to walk Zeke out. He grips his pocket, showing me that Ava has texted him so he needs to leave before my sister is raging at him for being late. They're like a married couple sometimes, without actual rings on their fingers. He says that I need to talk to Tem about things that have happened over the last year or so, but I honestly think he needs to talk to Ava as well, and finally make a full commitment to her.

I head into the kitchen to find Tem getting

ready to plate up the Chinese, with three bowls on the bench.

"Hey, is Zeke not staying?"

"Nah, Ava wants him home."

"Oh right, well more for us then. I got your fave."

"Satay chicken?"

"Yeah, with fried rice and beef with oyster as well," She says.

I hug her tightly, giving her a kiss.

"I love you, Temptress."

She kisses me back, and then replies, "I love you too, Simba. Let's go eat in front of the tv tonight."

"Sounds good," I reply, grabbing a plate and heaping it with food. Tem does the same and I follow her into the lounge room to watch Netflix, eat, and then hopefully chill later. I've missed being with her lately.

CHAPTER FOUR
Ezekiel

W hen I get home twenty minutes later I find Ava on the couch, clutching the throw rug.

Entering the room, I bend down and kiss her forehead.

"Hey firefly, you ok?"

"No Ezekiel. Where were you?"

I scoff under my breath, a little annoyed that she'd question me. "At Ashton's. Why?"

"Sure you were," she sasses me, sniffing back tears.

"Ava, come on, you know I wouldn't lie to you," I affirm, nodding at her. "Text Ash if you don't believe me."

She pouts, folding her arms across her chest.

She looks fucking sexy, but I don't dare say so or snigger. "I needed you home."

"I'm here now, firefly. What's wrong?" I question, leaning on the back of the couch.

She sniffs back more tears. "My period is starting. I have some spotting and really bad cramps."

My heart falls for her. My girl gets killer cramps every month, and she got so sick on the pill she had to go off it years ago. I'm scared as hell about knocking her up, partly because my best mate would surely kill me if I knocked up his 'little' sister, but I'm also not ready to be a dad.

But also curse using damn frangers when we fuck as well. I'll take the damn risk or pull out before I come rather than use a franger any day.

"Aww, firefly, I'm sorry."

She gives me a sweet smile, causing my heart to race when she murmurs, "It's ok, Zekey bear."

I love when Ava calls me that nickname. It's so cute and innocent when neither my girl nor I am.

It also makes me want to take care of my girl as well, especially when she's in pain.

"How about I run you a bath and we order in and watch some Netflix?" I suggest, kissing her forehead.

"Sounds good, Zekey bear," she muses softly, casting the throw rug aside to reveal she's only in a skimpy lace bralette and her high-waisted period knickers.

As she stands I pull her into my arms and she leans into my side as I help her to the bathroom.

Turning on the tap to warm, I squirt in Av's favourite strawberry bubble bath. She sighs, almost collapsing on the floor when I let go of her a moment. It breaks my heart every month seeing her so weak and in so much pain.

"Careful, firefly," I soothe, lifting her arms up to pull off the bra. Leaning down I kiss each of her nipples, and a jolt of pleasure rushes through her and she trembles in my arms as I grip her waist.

"Can you touch me, Zekey bear?" she asks, her eyes pleading with me. "You know that helps my cramps."

"Of course, firefly," I reply, shutting the water off and helping her climb into the steaming tub.

The water and bubbles come up to her waist, grazing her belly button and she murmurs softly. I sit down on the cold tile floor and lean forward to kiss her. She moans into the kiss.

"Zekey bear?" she questions my nickname against my lips.

"Yeah, firefly?"

"Can you get in with me?"

"Sure, firefly, scoot forward," I instruct her,

standing up and stripping off my t-shirt, jeans and boxers in record speed. I know my girl is in pain, but anytime I see her naked Z-man tents my daks, and admittedly I was hoping she'd ask me to get in with her. We can both get off, with me fingering her pussy whilst I rock my dick against her arse. We haven't tried anal yet–despite my asking her numerous times–but I desperately want to share that with her. We'd not been each other's first–both of us losing our virginity to others–because neither of us ever thought we'd get the chance to ever be together. I do still take pleasure in the fact I gave her her first orgasm though. When she rocked her wet pussy over my dick and covered me in the sweetness of her pussy for the first time after her mum got married again years ago, I was completely gone for Ava. I was already in love with her before that, since I was twelve and first noticed how pretty she was, but that night I re-alised the extent of my feelings. Ava will always be completely mine, the only girl–despite how many others I fucked before her–that I've ever and will ever love with my whole heart.

Climbing awkwardly into the bath, I stretch out my legs on either side of my girl, and grip her around the waist to yank her back to sit between my thighs. Her arse cheeks brush against my dick under the water, and I groan at how good it feels.

She tips her head back to kiss me, and I lick her lips to get her to open up for me. Letting me in, our tongues dance together and her lower body writhes, rocking in sweet torture against my aching dick. It seems like an age since we've fucked–or even given each other oral–and I'm bordering on desperate. Moving back to Lockgrove Bay a few months ago, just before Christmas had been so busy and we'd been so tired, that being together physically had taken a back burner. And now with Av's finally getting her period, after it being MIA for the last couple of months–from the stress I now know, thank fuck–sex is again off the cards for a week.

I'd be down for fucking her during shark week. Blood has never made me squeamish–and I'd fucked other girls during their rags–but Av's has voiced she's not down for that ride, so I don't push it with her. I'd rather fuck any other time of the month, so I can ravage her firstly with my tongue and then fuck her so hard she's screaming my name so loud the walls shake. I'm looking forward to fucking her in every room on every possible surface of our house and not having to worry about how loud we are. Granted having to be quiet whilst we fucked at uni–in case Ashton heard his sister screaming my name–was a turn on. But now I want to fuck Ava so hard she screams loud enough for the neighbours to hear.

She breaks our kiss with a moan, rasping against my lips, "Please touch me Zekey bear. I need to come."

I obey her request–because it's so damn sexy–sliding my hand from around her waist to her pussy beneath the water. "Lean back, Av's," I request, slowly rubbing her slit from the bottom up to her clit. She shivers at the touch, and I grip her neck to yank her back for a kiss as I slip a finger inside her pussy to finger fuck her.

She moans, rocking her hips, and her arse against my dick.

"Mmm, Zeke, feels so good," she moans loudly, my thumb brushing against her clit, flicking the sensitive bud.

"Come for me Ava," I groan into her ear, slipping another finger inside her and pumping them both in and out faster and harder, whilst still teasing her clit. She's still writhing in my lap, and I'm so close to coming myself.

Ava is moaning her pleasure, and I love hearing every moan and gasp that escapes her mouth whilst I make her feel good, whilst I take her pain away.

She starts to tremble, splashing water over the

edge of the bathtub as she curses, "Fuck, Ezekiel," as she comes hard.

Gripping her neck I tip her head back for a kiss, whispering against her pretty lips, "I love when you say my full name, Ava Darby."

She smiles at me, a sweet sexy smile when she taunts me, "Ezekiel Stefan." My name comes out husky, her voice strained with her still panting breaths from her orgasm.

"Fuck, Ava, fuck I love you."

"I love you too, Ezekiel," she tells me, kissing me again before she taunts me, "Your dick is really hard."

"You don't say," I taunt back, pushing my dick up into the curve of her arse. "Think you can make me come without touching me?"

She nods, laughing cheekily as she grips the side of the bathtub and starts to rock back and forth over my length. It's so damn tempting. I just want to slip inside her pussy and fuck her until there's no water left because it's all splashed over the sides. But I refrain. I'm too on edge anyway, and in mere minutes I'm shooting my load over Ava's arse and into the water.

"Damn, Av's, that was so hot," I tell her, leaning towards her and kissing her back. "Are you feeling better?"

"Yeah, the bath and orgasm helped a lot."

"I'm glad," I reply, helping her stand up with my arms around her. "Hop out, and we can go order pizza and snuggle in bed with Netflix on."

She climbs out, holding onto me for support. Following her out, I grab a towel and wrap it around her, helping her dry off before I hold out her knickers and she steps into them.

I give her a kiss on the forehead before we head to our bedroom.

She doesn't dress in anything else, climbing into bed and pulling the sheets up to her chin.

I grab some tight white boxers, slipping them on. I can feel Ava's eyes on me, and hear her moan.

"I love those boxers on you, Z," she confesses. I turn to face her, and kiss her again before I wiggle my hips to taunt her.

"You think I look sexy huh?"

"Yes, Zekey bear, but your birthday suit is sexier."

"Well, you can see that again later. We need food, and you need rest."

She nods and grabs her phone from the nightstand as I slide in beside her. She quickly orders our fave pizza for delivery, and I flick on Netflix, scrolling to our most recently watched. I put on an episode of *The Big Bang Theory* and pull Ava close.

I kiss her forehead, and smile at her, telling her, "I love you, Ava. I'm glad you're feeling better."

"I love you too, Ezekiel. Thank you for taking care of me."

"Anytime, firefly."

She snuggles in closer against my side, and she's asleep before the pizza arrives.

CHAPTER FIVE

Tempany

Sitting down on the couch, with Ashton by my side I yank the throw rug over my legs and put my plate of Chinese on my lap. He's flicking through the new shows and movies, but nothing piques our interest, so sighing he turns on 'Big Bang Theory'.

It's our comfort show, never failing to make us laugh, and that's just what I need right now. Just being together and eating dinner on the couch is just what we need.

I'm glad Zeke went home, as I need to speak to Ashton about what's been on my mind lately.

My stomach has been in knots, my mind a tumble of worry and thoughts. A wave of nausea hits me even now, and Ashton glances away from the TV, swallowing his mouthful of food and giving me a concerned look. A lopsided smile almost.

"Tem, you ok?" He asks, his voice wavering.

"Ar yeah, I just had a wave of nausea and I'm cramping a little."

He almost leaps off the couch, putting his Chinese down on the floor to rub my stomach. It's an odd reaction but I don't question him.

"Do you need to go to the hospital? " He questions, his voice full of panic.

"No. I'm fine. It's passed now, but I have been feeling more off lately," I admit as he sits back down on his side of the couch.

"Well maybe focus on the wedding planning instead. You know stress isn't good for you after everything."

"Yeah I know, and I'm not having any unusual bleeding so that is surely a good thing."

"Exactly, temptress," he says with a nod, and a hint of naughty in his voice when he says 'temptress'. "How about we finish up with this food, and head to bed. I can make you feel better then."

"Is that so, Simba?" I tease back, and he leans forward to kiss me sweetly.

"Yes, temptress. Your sexy simba will make you purr."

We finish our food in silence, except for

laughing occasionally at the TV. Ashton fusses and picks up our plates, not letting me even move until he's done cleaning the kitchen and putting away the leftovers.

Once he's done, he's back in the lounge room and flicks off the TV before scooping me up into his arms and carrying me to the bedroom. He puts me down on the bed and I scoot up to lean on the pillows, watching him as he undresses.

Climbing onto the bed—at the foot—he crawls towards me and lifts the hem of my dress to kiss my belly.

"I can't wait until your belly swells with our baby, Tem."

I sniff back tears, worried that I'll never be able to give Ashton the child he desperately wants. And it's not that I don't want a baby either, but with all my miscarriages I can't help but think it's never going to happen for us.

"Please don't say that Ashton. You know it might not happen for us."

He chuckles softly, tugging on my knickers and pulling them down my thighs.

"Let's just enjoy being together, Temptress."

I don't get a chance to respond before Ashton is parting my legs and pressing a kiss to my clit. His tongue laps at my entrance, darting his tongue in and out. I can't help but buck up my hips and moan. It feels so good, causing me to grip Ashton's hair as I let go and come all over his face. He stretches up over me to kiss me, and I lick my come from his lips, causing him to groan.

"I love it when you taste yourself on me, Tem."

"I love you, Ashton. Thanks for that, but I'm too tired for anything else tonight."

"That's ok, Temptress. Get some rest." He lays down beside me, tugging the sheets back and pulling them over us. I roll onto my side, and he pulls me close to spoon me. I feel his kiss on my temple, drifting to sleep before I can even say goodnight.

CHAPTER SIX

Ashton

The gym is buzzing with students, bouncing basketballs around the hardwood court for tryouts. It's odd being the coach seeing as I can put myself in the boys' shoes. I'd been in the exact same position as a lanky twelve-year-old. I'd only tried out for the Lockgrove Bay Lions team to piss my dad off and never expected to get onto the team, let alone be one of the top players ever. My high school basketball experience led me to the captaincy in my final year, and led me back here all these years later to be the coach. Coach Kinney had retired not long after I left for Uni, only filling in because he had to.

I probably could've come back earlier, but I didn't want to leave Tem alone in the city while finishing her teaching degree, and I also wanted my sports science degree under my belt — just in case.

The day I got the phone call from Principal Reading asking me to come back to coach the Lions I nearly choked on my beer. I'd almost not answered with the call coming through as a 'private' number. I don't know if I'd be here if I hadn't, earning a packet doing something I absolutely love. I'm in my element when doing anything related to basketball, and throwing a ball around and getting paid for it kinda feels like a stick it to my cunt of a father. Shooting a three-pointer, over and over, I feel elated, like I'm dancing on the fuckers grave and he's rolling in it.

Shaking thoughts of his hatred for me aside, I focus on the boys doing drills around me. There's some definite talent here, some boys that are shoe in's, and some I have to take regardless of their ball skills as they're scholarship students. Luckily those are few and far between, only three this year and they're decent players. Not captain material, but worth having on the team. My mind goes MIA for a moment, wondering if I ever have kids whether I'll have a basketballer and a legacy player on the team. I'm surprised there are no legacy kids this year, but they aren't commonplace. Drake 'DP' Peters would have a legacy kid, but he's not old enough to have a twelve-year-old, and last I heard he's somewhere overseas with his girlfriend Polly Baker. From what Lorena–Tempany's best friend and Polly's older sister–said, Drake had wanted to get as far from Lockgrove Bay as possible, to not have to see his old girlfriend everywhere. He was always a bit of a daft idiot, constantly falling for the wrong girls, and he was a shit player as well. But other than teasing him, there wasn't a thing I could do about it.

All that shit is in the past now though, we've all moved on, and I'm happy for the most part. Here at least, instilling my love of basketball in the next generation I'm happy, but there is still that ache for my own kids deep within my chest. I think it's because my father was such a cunt, a true arsehole, that I strived to never be and I want my own kids to grow up with a father who truly cares about them, who loves them no matter what and doesn't subject them to any of the abuse Ava and I were subjected to growing up.

Ava doesn't even know half of what he did to me, and she never will. It's always been my job to protect her and still is. Kinda.

She's got another protector now, and right now he's floating around the edge of the court, tossing the balls back in when the boys shooting throw them out of bounds.

I really don't need his help, but I get why he's here. The tosser is missing playing ball with me. It's been forever since we've played against each other, a tussle of one and one at the local park or beachside courts. But life and not living together anymore have gotten in the way.

His 'help' now is actually rather distracting, causing thoughts of the past to flash in my mind, like one afternoon on the outside court when I was sure he was fucking Ava and I completely lost it. I was adamant that something more had happened between them since they'd kissed on her sixteenth birthday. It hadn't, but the wanker was certainly in love with my little sister and now he's living with her, and her boyfriend. I try not to think about that, or anything to do with their relationship. I know he loves her, but he's still a dickwad–a hotheaded one–and I know I don't have to protect Ava, but I can't help it.

"Ezekiel, bro, don't you have somewhere else to be right now?" I question him, bouncing a ball towards him and aiming for his crotch.

"Nah, coach. I wanna help you out bro."

"I'm good," I tell him, dribbling the ball and running rings around him. My best mate is out of practice for sure. He tries to smack the ball out of my hands between bounces, but I'm too quick–too good–for him, and I turn my back to shoot for a three-pointer. The boys around me cheer and holler, "Way to go Coach Castello!"

Hearing that is like music to my ears. I'm the fucking coach, and my name precedes me. When I catch the ball from the return through the net, Zeke scoffs behind me. I turn back to him, taunting him, "Go back to the music room, Mr Alessio."

He gives me a snigger. "Well, if I'm not welcome to play b-ball with your majesty you could've just said so."

"Aww, poor Mr Alessio got his ego bruised," I tease him back, bouncing the ball towards him again. I let him intercept it this time, and he shoots and scores. His smile is devilish and he gives me an up yours as he heads out of the gym, yelling, "Later, Coach Castello! I'll whip your butt later!"

I could see he was going to say 'arse' but corrected himself at the last moment, and I snigger under my breath. Sometimes I wonder how in the hell he managed to become a teacher. He's insanely talented with his music and could have pursued a career in that but he chose to come home and fell into a job back in the stomping grounds of our high school. It's honestly good being back, as Lockgrove Bay is home.

CHAPTER SEVEN

Tempany

I t's been awhile since I've seen my best friend.

Being back in the bay has meant I've seen her more but with me starting work and Lo running around with her two kids—whilst her husband Beau runs their mechanic business—it's been tough to organise a time to see each other. Feeling like I've been hit by a bus all the time lately hasn't exactly helped either.

But finally, we're having a lunch date. I'm a little early so I slide into a seat at a small table in Melba's to wait for her. I glance around the small coffee shop, loving the old school, quaint decor they have going on. Melba's has been the local go-to coffee shop since the eighties and it hasn't changed a bit. It's special and loved by locals and tourists alike. I can't help but think about when I came here for Ariel & Dakota's surprise baby shower. It wasn't long after I'd had my second miscarriage and it was hard keeping it together and being happy for them both. Now, things have changed with Ariel having her two kids Bria and Kyler, and helping Briston and Jebediah in having their son Isaiah plus trying to get her art gallery up and running. All our lives are so busy, so it's no wonder we don't get to see each other. I honestly only really see Ava because she's practically my sister in law and my step mum insists on family dinners every fortnight on a Sunday. They're still hella awkward with Ashton and Ezekiel still not completely on the same team with Zeke being with Ava. I think Zeke has more than proven he's in it with Ava for the long haul, but without a ring on her finger Ashton will forever think his best friend is going to break his little sister's heart.

The over the door bell jangles and the people entering are excitedly chatting. Glancing towards the door, I see it's Lorena, and she has Grady and Lucy with her. She looks completely frazzled and sighs as she slides into the seat across from me. Pulling Grady onto her lap, she apologises, "Sorry I had to bring them with me, Te, but hey."

"Hey, Lo," I reply, pulling an extremely excited

Lucy closer to me on the bench seat I'm sitting on.

"And it's fine Lo. I love being Auntie Te."

"I appreciate that, Tem," Lorena replies, grabbing a menu from the middle of the table. "At least let me buy your lunch."

"You don't have to do that, Lo," I tell her.

"I want to, Tempany."

"Ok, well, I'll have a chicken caesar salad," I say without even having to open the menu. They're the best and I'm kinda craving one, as well as milk.

"And a drink?" Lorena questions.

"I'd love a choc mint milkshake," I respond, not able to hide my giddy smile.

""No worries," she replies, standing and helping Grady off his seat. Holding his hand they go up to the counter to order.

Grady is jumping around, a bundle of energy. I honestly don't know how Lorena does it, with two kids under four.

Lucy shifts next to me, and I touch her pretty pink tutu dress.

"Have you been doing ballet, Lucy?"

"Yeah, I in with Ms. C. She pretty."

I'm surprised by her vocabulary considering she's just turned two but clearly having an older brother who doesn't shut up—except when sleeping—makes a difference.

"That's great you're in Ms. Castello's class," I tell her with a smile. "Do you like ballet?"

Ava has started teaching ballet classes at the local dance school. It's not something I thought she'd do but she's enjoying it.

"Yes, love it," Lucy beams as Lorena and Grady come back to the table. Lucy glares at her mum. I want to discipline her for that but it's not my place.

"Nuggies, mummy?"

"Yes, Lucy, I ordered you nuggets and chips."

Lucy huffs. "I don't want hips."

"You will eat them, Lucy Irene."

She huffs again, and folds her arms across her chest. I fight the urge to laugh, looking down at the table.

But then I hear Lorena laugh and burst out laughing myself. "Normal reaction, I'm guessing?"

"Every day, Te. But nuggets are life."

"Yeah they so are," I reply, smiling wide at my best friend.

"So how's things with you?" She asks, touching my hands that are resting on the table.

"Ok. Work is going well, but I've been feeling really off lately," I admit. She doesn't get to reply straight away as our food is brought to the table. Immediately I slurp down a few big gulps of my milkshake. It's delicious and hits the spot.

"Taste good?"

"So good,"I mumble, taking another sip and adding after I swallow, "I've been craving milk so much lately."

Lorena practically gapes at me. "You're not pregnant are you?"

I scoff, not wanting to even think of that being a possibility but also knowing it could be.

"I... um, don't think so," I confess, taking a forkful of my salad into my mouth.

"Well, have you had any other odd symptoms?"

"I've been cramping a bit, and I haven't had my period in a couple months."

Lorena's eyes light up, and a wave of nausea hits me. "Well, have you taken a test?" She asks, her tone hopeful.

I shake my head, stabbing another lettuce leaf. "No, I'm too scared, Lo."

"That makes sense, but don't you also want to know so you can prepare?"

I sniff back the tears now stinging my eyes. "If I don't find out, and I lose the baby again, it might not hurt as much."

"That's BS, Tempany," Lorena shrieks. "You need to take a test."

I nod, replying, "I know, Lo."

We eat in silence then, except for her kids that

are munching on their nuggets—and chips—loudly, despite Lucy's protest of eating them. The nausea has bubbled up again, and I really don't want to eat anymore, but I force myself and hope it doesn't come back up later to taunt me. In my head I know Lorena is right. I'm probably pregnant, but my heart doesn't want to believe it. It's the guiding force blocking out the pain of my miscarriages. But I feel different this time, and I need to find out for myself.

CHAPTER EIGHT

Ashton

Tempany has been acting odd lately, telling me one moment she's feeling sick, and the next she's horny as hell and jumping me any chance she gets. We'd fucked on the kitchen counter this morning, and I had to book it hard in the Mustang to get us to work on time. The look she kept giving me on the way to work almost had me calling in sick, but once we arrived she got out of the car and promised to come over for lunch as she didn't have play support or her class after lunch break.

IT'S LUNCH NOW, AND I'M GULPING DOWN A couple of slices of pizza whilst watching the door, eager to see my temptress arrive.

Zeke elbows me in the side.

"Why're you looking at the door like that, bro?"

I scoff down my final bites of pizza and respond, "Like what, dickwad?"

"I don't know. Like it's some magical teleportation barrier beyond or something."

I glare at him, and then laugh, hard, because that is some weird shit he just blurted out.

"Zeke, dude, are you drunk? High?"

"I wish, Ash," he remarks, laughing. "But I'm a good boy at school."

"You're never a good boy, Ezekiel," I taunt my best friend, laughing so hard.

His gaze shifts back to the door, and then to me when he says with a teasing tone, "And your woman just arrived, so I'm thinking the only naughty one around here is you, Ashton."

I stand and give Zeke an up yours. We're grown men now, but some things never change. We act like our teenage selves most days.

Ignoring his taunts from behind me, I step closer to Tem and yank her into my arms to kiss her.

I hear Zeke holler from behind us. "Get a room!"

Again behind my back, I give him an up yours

before breaking the kiss with Tempany and dragging her out of the staff room.

As I tug her down the corridors I swear I can everyone staring at us, giving us glares as though they know I'm about to fuck her on my desk if I have my way.

We sneak into my office, and closing the door I lock it with the snib, and draw down the blinds so no one can see into—or barge into—my office without warning.

Tempany giggles and shoves me backwards towards my desk, kissing me so hard I gasp for breath.

"Damn, temptress," I gasp breaking the kiss, and gripping her waist to spin her around, causing her butt to hit the edge of my desk.

"Fuck me, Ashton," she requests, biting down on her lip.

Again gripping her waist I sit her up on the edge of the desk, and pry her legs open, thankful she's wearing a dress today. Lifting the hem up and tucking the fabric up I admire the lacy knickers she's wearing and the wet patch on the crotch. She seems a little more bloated than usual but I don't say anything about it. Now is not the time to mention her weight.

Instead, I slide a finger into the top of her

knickers, brushing a digit over her clit causing her to gasp.

"Ashton..." she moans, licking her lips and bucking her hips up towards my palm as I slip a finger inside her pussy to find she's insanely wet.

"Damn, temptress you're so turned on for me."

She nods, rocking her hips more as I finger her, sliding two fingers in and out of her wet pussy with my thumb brushing over her clit.

"Yes, Ashton, fuck...more," she demands, gasping for a breath.

"Want me to fuck you, here on my desk temptress?" I ask, stilling my fingers inside her and kissing her.

"Yes, Simba," she purrs at me, smirking.

I don't waste a moment, pulling my fingers out and slipping them between my lips to taste her before I tug her underwear down. They fall to the floor at my feet and I follow them, dropping to my knees in front of her and prying her legs open even more.

She's so wet I can see her pussy glistening with arousal.

Leaning forward I lick her clit, causing her to moan so loudly I'm sure the whole school could hear her.

I don't stop her though, trailing my tongue between her folds and darting it inside her, tasting her arousal and lapping it up. Her hips buck and she begins to pant, breathy *'fucks'* escaping her lips whilst I fuck her with my tongue.

It's been ages since I've gone down on her, and quite frankly I've missed it, the taste of her on my tongue.

It's barely a minute before she's clutching the desk, her fingers turning white as she climaxes all over my tongue.

Standing up I rip my belt open and yank my slacks and boxers to my ankles.

Grabbing Tempany's waist I move her back on the desk, and pry her legs open, stepping in between them, lining my dick up with her pussy. I push inside her, pumping in and out, causing her to moan rather loudly, however, I don't silence her.

I could lose my job for this—if someone hears us—but I don't care.

Making Tempany come—making her happy—is all that matters.

It's only a few minutes before I'm letting go, and filling her pussy with my load.

Pulling out, I step back and grab her knickers from the floor. She scoots off the edge of the desk and tugs them up her legs under her dress. I pull my daks up, awkwardly tucking my junk back into my tight slacks.

Tempany smiles at me, kissing me on the cheek.

"Thanks for an epic fuck, Simba. I'm feeling so much better now."

"That's good, Tem. I'll see you after work."

"You've got training until five, right?"

"Yeah, I'll come get you from your classroom when we're done."

"Ok, sounds great. I can catch up on admin."

She gives me a sweet kiss, then unlatches the door lock and leaves my office.

I open the blinds again, and sit down to work through the game statistics ready for training.

I'm still not sure what to make of Tem's sudden behaviour change towards sex. But at the same time I'm not going to complain.

What sane man would?

CHAPTER NINE
Ava

Briston and Jeb's house is full of Christmas decorations and practically everyone from our year level at school, and some others like Ashton and Tempany are here for the party as well.

Christmas music is playing and everyone is chatting, eating canapé type foods and drinking.

Tempany is glancing around the room as she leans against the kitchen counter. She doesn't look at all excited to be here, and honestly looks really pale.

Stepping up to her, I smile and give her a hug which she accepts. She sniffs back a sob when breaking the hug.

"You ok, sis?" I ask, noticing that she doesn't have a drink in hand like most people.

"Yeah, I'm just tired. Work has been hard since going back after the holidays."

"Yeah, I bet. Ballet classes have been intense too," I acknowledge. "But you know you can talk to me anytime, about anything."

"I know, Av's," she responds, again sniffing back sobs, her gaze shifting to Ariel across the room by the Christmas tree.

It is odd that Tempany's not drinking. Usually at things like this she would. It makes me wonder if she's pregnant. Tempany and Ashton have been trying for a baby for at least a year and it's not happening. I feel horrible for them both. I can't honestly imagine what that would be like, especially when it's something you want so much.

"I'm going to go find Ash," Tempany informs me. I watch her walk away, her glare still on Ariel. I grab a drink then, taking a sip of the cool beer.

Without warning it's snatched from my grip and I turn to find my boyfriend behind me. He puts the cup down on the counter and wraps an arm around me from behind.

"You look sexy tonight, firefly," he whispers teasingly in my ear. His voice sends a shiver through me. I turn in his arms and kiss him, stretching up on my tiptoes. He moans into the kiss, pressing his hips into mine.

"Wanna sneak away for a quickie, Zekey bear?" I ask raspily against his lips.

"As much as I'd love to ravage you right now firefly I don't think sneaking off in our friend's house is right."

I huff at him, but I know he's right, even though it's an odd response for Zeke.

"Fine Zekey bear, you're right. But when we get home tonight, you better make it up to me."

"Oh I will, Ava, I will," he promises, giving me another kiss.

He gives my butt a playful slap and walks away. I watch him a moment before I grab my drink and head over to Ariel.

"Hey Ar's."

"Hi Av's," she responds, smiling at me. "You and Zeke seem great."

"Yeah, but he turned me down for a sneaky quickie."

"Oh, that doesn't sound like him."

"I know but I get it. How's it being married to Brae?"

"Different, but it's good. I love when he calls me Mrs Chappell."

"Sounds so dirty. He really loves you, Ar's."

"Yeah, I know, and he's such a good dad."

"Yeah, are you enjoying your night away from the kids?"

"Kinda," she replies, laughing. "I miss them a lot but I'm excited about spending some dirty time with my guys later." She blushes with the words and I squeal.

"Seriously? You're going to have a foursome?"

"Yeah, with Brae, Bris and Jeb."

"Damn girl, that's so hot. You're so damn lucky."

"Yeah, love is better shared. I love Brae so much, but I'll always love Bris as well," she admits, blushing again.

"Yeah, that makes sense. I know Bris loves Jeb a lot but he's always loved you, even when he didn't realise it."

"Zeke's always loved you too. Have you guys talked about getting married? Kids?"

"No, not really. I'm sure he wants kids, but we haven't talked about it and with Ash and Tem trying for a baby and it not happening for them I'd hate to take the joy of Ashton giving mum the first grandchild away."

"That's a tough one for sure. What about you getting married?"

"I'd marry him yesterday, but I want him to ask me."

Ariel nods. "Yeah, makes sense."

"I'm a traditional girl," I say with a laugh.

Ariel laughs as well and then responds, "I was

until I fell in love with two boys and got pregnant."

"But you wouldn't take anything back, right?"

"Never. I love Braeden and my babies more than anything."

Speaking of her husband, he's sauntering across the room and he only has eyes for her as he gives her a passionate kiss, sweeping her into his arms and dipping her low.

Breaking the kiss, he murmurs, "Hey darling."

Even I can admit that the way Braeden says darling is ridiculously sexy.

"Hey, Brae," Ariel responds, stumbling a little as he settles her back on her feet. Braeden turns to me. "Hey Av's. Having fun?"

"Always, Brae, and don't worry your wife only has good things to say about you." I give him a wink.

"Good to know," He replies, smiling

I nod, pressing my lips together as I head off, leaving them to get lost in kissing each other whilst I go to find my boyfriend again. Talking to Ariel has definitely made me want it all with Zeke. I know he loves me, but I'm ready to commit completely to the guy. We've been together for five years, but I've been in love with Ezekiel Alessio since I was a kid.

He's my forever.

CHAPTER TEN
Tempany

While I'm happy for Briston and Jebediah getting married, I'm not happy being at their wedding. It's making me long for my wedding to Ashton to be here sooner.

My emotions have been all over the place as of late, with being on the verge of tears a lot. I love my job but being around kids all day, five days a week, is breaking my heart. The thought of never having kids of my own just tears me apart. I want a daughter to do all the things with her that I never got to do with my mum. Dressing her up in pretty dresses, braiding her beautiful long hair, playing dolls with her. I want it all and I'm scared I'm never going to get it.

The wedding ceremony was utterly beautiful,

the vows the guys exchanged so heartfelt I'd choked back gasps of breath as I cried.

Ashton had taken my hand and smiled at me to let me know he was by my side. I'm so lucky to have Ashton as my fiancé. Our getting together was a long road, with all the things that happened with our parents, becoming step-siblings and crossing the forbidden line to fall in love. If his mum and my dad hadn't been supportive of us loving each other I would've been a wreck. Ashton is most definitely my forever. My protector.

At the reception now I'm sitting at a table I'm sharing with Ava, Zeke, Ashton, and some other guys I don't know, who must be friends of Jeb's or possibly from their year level that I don't remember. Because Ava is pretty much my sister now and she's with Zeke I sometimes forget she's a year younger than me, and two years younger than Ashton.

Glancing around the room I notice Ariel talking to and dancing with her kids. She's so carefree, and the kids are so happy. Bria is an absolute doll, and Kyler is the cutest little boy I've ever seen. It causes my heart to ache, and I'm quite frankly jealous of seeing Ariel with her kids. Ashton notices my unease and taps my shoulder.

"Temptress, what's getting you down?" he asks, genuine concern on his face.

I nod towards Ariel discreetly. "It hurts seeing Ariel with her kids."

"I know, Tem. But it will happen for us soon. I'm sure of it." His voice is slightly raised and Ava overhears.

"You'll get to be a mum, Tem. I know you will."

"Thanks, Av's. I hope so, but each month that goes by without being pregnant gets me down more and more."

I sniff back tears, and Ashton wraps his arm around my waist. He doesn't say a word, just kisses my cheek. He's been my rock through all the miscarriages, giving me all the support and love I could ask for. And now is no different. With the way I'm feeling at the moment, I'm crossing my fingers, my toes, my everything, that our time is here. And if I *am* pregnant, I'm worried about miscarrying again and think it's best to hide anything from Ashton, just in case. He might hate me, but it's for the best.

CHAPTER ELEVEN

Tempany

In the bathroom, I'm staring at the tiny white stick in my hand in utter disbelief. It's showing me two blazing pink lines, the second one so vivid it's pulling colour from the control line. I'm pregnant and probably a lot further along than I'm thinking.

I blank out for a moment, sinking to the floor and resting my back against the toilet bowl. Knocking on the door startles me, and my best friend's voice is eager. "Te, did you take it?"

"Ah, yeah. I just...need a minute," I stammer.

"Well, let me in. I can wait with you."

I stand, a little unsteady on my feet and open the door for Lorena. Tears are starting to stream down my cheeks. It's a mix of emotions. I'm happy to be pregnant again, but I'm also terrified it will end in a loss as it has before.

"Te, are you ok?" Lorena asks, leaning against the sink. "Is it negative?"

"No. It's positive, Lo. I'm pregnant."

Her face lights up. "That's awesome Te! Congrats are in order." My best friend wraps her arms around me in a tight hug, causing me to drop the test to the ground. I sniff back my tears as we break the hug.

"Are you not happy about it?"

"Of course I am, but I'm scared, Lo. I don't want to tell Ashton."

Lorena shakes her head. "I don't think keeping this from him is a good idea, Te. He deserves to know."

"I have to, Lo. If I miscarry again, it will break his heart. I can't do that to him again."

"I guess, but don't keep it from him too long. That will break his heart just as much."

Nodding at my best friend, I pick up the test, the box, and the wrapper and we leave my bathroom. My heart is still racing as I log in to arrange a doctor's appointment for tomorrow.

I COULDN'T GET AN APPOINTMENT AT THE doctor for after school, so I ended up going home early from work. I'd had to tell Ashton that I was meeting Lorena, so we'd drive separately. I hate lying to him, but I know it's for the best. At least for now.

The doctor confirms my pregnancy with another test and arranges an ultrasound for a couple of weeks away when he believes I'll be about six or seven weeks. Leaving the doctor, I push open the door and bump straight into Ariel who's also leaving.

"Hey Ariel," I greet her, glancing down at her belly.

"Hi, Tempany. What're you doing here?"

"I um...had to confirm something."

"Oh, are you feeling ok?"

"Not really, but given the circumstances, it's expected to be a little under the weather."

"Tell me about it," Ariel replies with a laugh. "Wanna go grab a coffee?"

"Sounds great," I respond, following her down the street towards Melba's. I didn't have much to do with Ariel at school, with her being in the year below me, but she's good friends with Ava and Dakota so she's been around more recently. I can tell she's been finding things tough with Braeden being on tour with his band the B-boys and having to look after her two kids.

Once inside Melba's, we order coffee, and Ariel smiles at me.

"So what's got you down?"

"I'm...um...just found out I'm pregnant, and I'm scared of miscarrying again."

"Oh wow, congrats, Tempany," she responds, her smile wider. "But yeah it's scary for sure. I haven't told anyone but I had an early miscarriage before this pregnancy and it nearly broke Bris and Jeb's hearts."

I gape at her. "You're pregnant?"

"Yeah, I'm about three, nearly four months along as a surrogate for Bris and Jeb."

"That's wonderful, Ariel. I'm happy for you and the boys. That's really special."

"Thanks. I just found out I'm having a boy. I can't wait to tell Bris and Jeb."

I finish the rest of my coffee and excuse myself before heading home. I want to be home before Ashton and the whole drive I'm hoping he doesn't ask any questions about how I'm feeling, as I'm not sure how long I'll be able to keep things hidden as it is. I'm getting more morning sickness, and I'm extremely bloated. I'll be showing before I know it. But at least by that point, I should be in the clear to tell him.

CHAPTER TWELVE

Ashton

Sitting on the edge of our bed, I'm holding the box of pregnancy tests in one hand and the clearly positive—and quite possibly months old—test in my other hand. My mind is going around in circles thinking the worst with how Tempany has been acting lately.

We hadn't had any pregnancy tests or baby items in the house since moving back to Lockgrove Bay, so finding these in the bottom drawer in the bathroom when looking for a new tube of toothpaste has me baffled, confused, and angry. I've been getting the sense she's been hiding something from me, but I never would have expected her to hide being pregnant.

She'd told me today she had a doctor's appointment so we went to work separately, but still I didn't even think to question her or demand to go with her. I can be a hothead, but I've never been that guy who controls the woman I'm with by attending appointments or prying into every little thing in her life.

I hear her unlock the front door, her sweet voice calling out, "Ash, I'm home."

I gulp down the lump in my throat, about to stand up from the bed to go and confront her when she walks into the bedroom. She's shucking off her high heels and smiles at me.

"Oh hey, you are home."

"Of course, I'm home, Tempany. It's nearly six," I bellow at her, angry at myself for my raised tone of voice.

I can't hide it though, and squeeze the box in my hand to try and calm myself which Tempany notices, her gaze dropping to the test in my hand. She gasps, moving across the bedroom to the walk-in robe to change.

"Tempany?" I question, my voice loud.

She pokes her head out. "Yeah?"

I hold up the test. "When did you take this?"

She gulps hard. "Um...like a month or so ago."

I stand, stalking towards her, dropping the box and test on the floor on the way over.

"And when did you plan on telling me?"

"I don't know. Soon."

"Come on Tempany. You should have said something before you even took a test."

"I'm scared Ashton. I didn't want to miscarry again, and have you go through that all again." She's sobbing through her words.

"That's not fair. I'd support you, Tem. I'm your fucking fiancé. Don't you think I deserve to know that you're pregnant with my baby?"

"Of course you do. But I just wanted to wait until I was further along, that's all."

"That's bullshit. You deliberately hid it from me. It's probably not even my kid." The moment the words leave my mouth and I see her shocked expression, I regret the outburst.

She loudly sobs, shoving her hands against my chest.

"How can you say that, Ashton!" She screams at me. "I can't believe you'd even think I'd cheat on you just to have a baby."

"I'm sorry, I'm just upset that you hid it from me."

"That doesn't give you the right to call me a cheater. I would never do that."

"I..I...I'm sorry, Tem. I just thought the worst."

Stepping back she picks up a gym bag from the pile on the floor.

"What're you doing with that?"

"I'm leaving for a bit. I can't be around you right now."

She starts shoving clothes into the bag, sobbing and sniffing back tears.

"Come on Tem, please don't leave. I said I was sorry," I tell her, reaching out to touch her arm.

"Don't Ashton. Just leave me alone."

I walk away and sit on the edge of the bed again. Watching her pack a bag and then walk out of our bedroom without another word breaks my heart. I should've kept my damn mouth shut and kept the peace. Now I don't even know if she'll come back, and I honestly don't even know if she's actually pregnant or if she has miscarried again. I hear the front door slam with her leaving and collapse back onto the bed, tears stinging my cheeks. I've fucked up.

CHAPTER THIRTEEN

Tempany

Pounding on my best friend's door, I inhale gulps of air whilst waiting for her to answer. I'd texted her on the way over but she hadn't replied. I'm hoping that coming to her is ok. Her life is busy with her kids, work, and supporting Beau with the workshop.

The door swings open, and it's Beau standing in front of me with Lucy on his hip.

"Oh hi, Tempany. You ok, love?" Beau asks, putting Lucy down as he ushers me inside.

"Um, yeah, kinda. I texted Lo but she didn't reply."

He nods, closing the door behind me.

"She's on her way home from the city. Went on a bit of a shopping spree for the kids."

"Oh, ok. I can go. I don't want to intrude." I sniff back tears. I'm upset about my fight with Ashton and need my best friend. I also don't know where else I can go right now either.

"You aren't intruding, Tempany. You can stay until Lorena gets home."

"Thanks, I...don't know where else to go right now," I mumble, following Beau into the kitchen.

"You're always welcome here," Beau says with a welcoming tone. My best friend found a great guy and has two amazing kids because of him. She took on Beau's son Grady like he was her own and I truly think that's selfless. I've thought about adoption or fostering but I long for my own kids. I touch my stomach, rubbing it softly and silently praying for this baby to be alright. For this time to be mine. For my chance to finally be a mum.

"Would you like a coffee or tea?"

I nod, taking a seat on the breakfast bar stool as a rush of dizziness hits me.

"A tea would be lovely," I croak out. Beau makes our drinks, and I scroll on my phone for a moment, looking at the pictures of Ashton and me on my Instagram. He made me so upset and angry with his words today but I still love him with all my heart and I honestly don't want to do this without him.

I'm tempted to go back home, but at the same

time, I can't face him yet. Beau puts a cup of tea in front of me and I only get to take a small sip when I hear my best friend's voice.

"Beau, baby. I'm home."

Lorena enters the kitchen and hugs her husband. He kisses her forehead. The sweet gesture makes me smile.

Lorena looks at me. "Hey Te, sorry I didn't get a chance to reply to your message. Are you ok?"

I take a few more sips of my tea before I reply. "I need a place to stay for a day or so. And to talk."

"Of course, Te. You can stay as long as you need. And you're in luck about talking, as it's Beau's night to cook dinner."

I stand from the stool and follow my best friend into the living room. We sit on opposite ends of the couch.

Lorena touches my leg comfortingly. "So bestie, what's going on?"

Sighing, I reply, "I fought with Ashton."

"What about?"

"He found out about my pregnancy and got angry because I didn't tell him. He accused me of cheating."

"Sounds like he was just upset, and honestly Te I told you so. You shouldn't have hidden it from him."

"I know that now, but his reaction hurt a lot. I needed some space."

Lorena nods. "That makes sense. You're welcome to stay here, but maybe it's not the best place for you right now."

I give her a confused look. "I don't understand, Lo."

"I think you need family right now. And being around my kids will only cause you to be upset, Tempany."

"I love being around your kids though."

"I know, but I can also see that being around my kids is hard for you. Go to your dad's and speak to him and your stepmum about everything."

"I don't know if I'm ready to tell them. It still really hurts talking about everything."

Lorena gasps at me. "Do they really not know about what you've been through?"

"No. They only know we've been trying for a baby."

"Then you, my girl, need to go and tell them now."

I sniff back the silent tears that have started to stain my cheeks. "Ok I will, but I'm putting it on you if it all goes bad." I point at her.

"It won't, Tempany."

"I'm trusting you, Lo," I tell her, standing up from the couch. She follows and hugs me. Not saying anything else but a goodbye to Beau, I leave and head for my parents' house.

CHAPTER FOURTEEN
Ashton

Bringing the bottle of beer to my lips, I flop down on the couch, gulping down the last few mouthfuls before I launch the bottle at the wall. It shatters, causing a loud crash reverberating around the empty lounge room—the empty *house*. Not having Tempany here is breaking my heart, but I'm also angry with her for hiding her pregnancy from me. I'm scared as well, but the upset outweighs that right now. I can't even think straight, feeling like I'm spiralling out of control. All I want to do is drink myself stupid so I don't have to feel anything.

I can't believe I was such an idiot and accused Tempany of cheating on me. I know she'd never cheat on me, just as I would never cheat on her.

The very thought of that is heart-shattering. I'd never even think of doing that. I've never cheated on a girl and I never will. And Tempany isn't just a girl, she's my everything, my fiancee'. She's my dream girl, and no one will ever compare to her, be her, or replace her if we're over. I let out a wail from letting the thought of replacing her enter my mind. I could never. I've been in love with Tempany since I was eight when she played basketball with me. Yeah, I blamed her for everything that happened with my father, but I knew it wasn't her fault. Fidel Castello was an arsehole, and nothing I did or didn't do would've changed that.

I didn't give a rat's arse when he died in jail, offed himself. He deserved that end, although he honestly took the easy way out. I felt no pain then, only a sense of relief, but living life without my temptress in it—just the thought of that—causes me unfathomable pain. I don't even want to think about that.

I'm just waiting for her to walk through the door, any minute, any day now. It's only been forty-eight hours, but it feels like a lifetime and looks like months with the number of beer bottles and pizza boxes strewn across the lounge room. I also stink as I haven't showered or stepped foot in our bedroom since Tem left. It smells like her in our bedroom, and that just makes me want to cry. I'm going to stay right here on the couch until my temptress returns. Fuck going to work. Fuck life. It's not worth living with Tempany by my side.

CHAPTER FIFTEEN

Tempany

I honestly don't think I've ever been so nervous. This time around going to an ultrasound is causing me so much anxiety. Hopefully, it's third time lucky and this pregnancy will stick. If my violent morning sickness is anything to go by, then I'm definitely still pregnant.

"I'm so nervous," I tell Lorena, who's holding the door of the medical centre open, pushing me inside.

"You'll be fine, Tem. I have a feeling this is your time."

"I hope so. I can't deal with another heartbreak."

She nods but doesn't respond, pushing me towards the reception desk. The receptionist gets me to fill out a form, and I sit next to Lorena in the waiting room. I bounce my knees, trying to calm myself. Lorena rests her hand on my knee.

"Te, you need to calm down. Stressing out isn't good for the baby."

"I know," I respond, turning to look at my best friend. "Thanks for being here with me."

"Anytime, but I wish you'd have bought Ashton with you. You need to be sharing this."

"I can't right now, Lo."

"Have you spoken to him?"

"No. Maybe after the ultrasound when I know things are good."

Before Lorena can reply, my name is called. She doesn't get up, but I take her hand and pull her up to drag her with me. I need to hold someone's hand when the bad news hits me again.

Once in the room, the scanning technician gets me to lie down on the bed. Lorena stands by the bed, and I take her hand in mine after lifting my t-shirt to expose my stomach. I'm definitely bloated, or maybe I'm showing early this time. I gasp when the cold gel hits my stomach. It causes my heart to race.

"Well, no wonder you've been so unwell, Tempany," The ultrasound tech says.

Again I gasp, asking, "Why? What's wrong?"

"You're having twins and all appears to be fine. You're about eight weeks along."

I let myself glance at the screen to see two blobs wiggling around in what appears to be two sacks.

"Oh wow. Twins. Can you tell if they're identical or fraternal?" I ask, still in awe of what I'm seeing on the screen.

The technician nods, pointing at the screen. "They're fraternal as there are two sacks."

I look at Lorena, squeezing her hand. "I'm having twins, Lo."

"Yeah, Te. So exciting. Makes up for the struggle you've had getting pregnant."

The technician finishes up the scan and closes the machine down. I pull my top down after she wipes the gel off my stomach and Lorena helps me up.

As we walk out I can't wipe the smile off my face. I'm having twins and all is well so far with my pregnancy. I've never gotten further along than six weeks, so another two weeks along gives me hope that this is finally my time. I need to tell Ashton, but I'm not ready to face him.

CHAPTER SIXTEEN

Ashton

The bashing on my front door startles me from whatever drunken stupor I'd put myself in. I honestly don't know what day it is, nor what time of the day it is. There is daylight flooding the room though, through the open curtains that I haven't closed since Tempany left.

A bellowing voice accompanies the bashing. "Open the fucking door, Ashton!"

It's Zeke, and he's pissed. He never calls me Ashton. Stumbling off the couch, I trip over the beer bottles scattered over the floor, cursing when I nearly fall flat on my face. Fumbling I unlock the door, and the second I open it Zeke barges in.

He screws up his nose in disgust. "Fuck, eww,

Ash, it smells like someone damn near died in here."

"Might as well be dead," I mumble, staggering back towards the couch.

"Why? What the hell is going on?"

"Tem fucking left me Zeke. Told me she's pregnant and fucking left me."

His mouth falls open. "Tem's pregnant?"

"Yes, arsehole. And she left me."

"Tem wouldn't leave you for no reason," Zeke says, his tone flat.

I flop back down on the couch, and Zeke stands at the armrest. "Well, I um..."

"You what, dickhead?"

"I accused her of cheating on me."

Zeke scoffs, laughing loudly.

"You're a *fucking idiot*, Ashton. Tem would never cheat on you."

"I know that!" I snap. "But I was upset that she didn't tell me she was pregnant and I found out when I saw the pregnancy test in the bin."

"I agree that she should've told you, but that doesn't explain your bullshit reaction."

"Yeah, I'm a dickhead, but it doesn't matter now. She's gone."

"Come on Ash man, are you seriously being a daft dickhead right now?"

"What the fuck do you mean?" I ask, looking up at him.

"Where do you think Tem would've gone?"

"I don't know. For all I know she's in Timbuktu."

"You really are being an idiot. She's probably at your parent's house. She would still have to go to work, unlike some people who skipped out the last few days."

I stand up from the couch and usher Zeke out the door. He reluctantly leaves, giving me a death glare as I shut the door in his face.

Quickly I clean up my mess, shovelling all of my mess into a garbage bag ready to take out to the bin. I grab the disinfectant spray from the kitchen and wipe down the coffee table before I have a quick shower to freshen up.

After dressing, I rush out the door, gunning it over to my parents house.

When I arrive, I barge in without even knocking—thankful that the front door is rarely locked—finding mum in the kitchen cooking dinner. I must look like I'm irate, due to the clenching of my fists.

"Darling, calm down. What's wrong?"

My voice comes out all caveman—croaky and demanding, "Where is she?"

Mum smiles and replies calmly, "In her old room."

I head up the stairs, inhaling some deep breaths to calm myself before I knock on Tempany's old bedroom door.

I hope she forgives me.

CHAPTER SEVENTEEN

Tempany

There's a soft knocking on my bedroom door. I don't have a clue who's behind the door, but even so I call out, "Come in!"

The door swings open and Ashton saunters into my room, his eyes locking on me sitting on the bed reading. I'm only in a short lace nightie that I found in my drawer, and I know with my legs crossed Ashton can clearly see my underwear.

He smiles, sitting down on the edge of the bed. "Hey Temptress."

I smile back, not able to hide my feelings from him. I've missed him so much, and seeing him right in front of me has lust stirring inside my stomach. I've honestly never touched myself to orgasm so many times in my life than I have the last couple of days.

"Hi Ashton," I respond, my voice scratchy. "What are you doing here?"

He takes my hand, causing me to throw my book on the bed. I should be annoyed as I don't remember what page I was up to, but his touch sends shivers through me, right down to my core.

"I missed you Tem, but I thought you didn't want to see me, and I didn't know where you were. It wrecked me."

"I missed you too, Ashton. But you really hurt me, and I needed some space."

"I know. I never should have reacted that way about you being pregnant. I just panicked."

I squeeze his hand, replying softly, "I panicked too, but this time it's real Simba."

"Have you been for an ultrasound? Heard the heartbeat?"

I nod, grinning when I respond, "Heartbeats."

He gapes, squeezing my hand tighter in his grip. "What? More than one baby?"

"Yeah, Simba. We're having twins."

"Oh my god, Temptress, that's amazing," he bellows, leaning forward and grabbing my neck to yank me closer. Before I can even respond he's kissing me, hard and full of pent up lust from not seeing each other for nearly a week. It's not a forgiving kiss, nor a punishing kiss. It's a kiss that shows all of his emotions.

I murmur against his mouth, and he involves tongue, pushing me down onto the pillows behind me. Still kissing me, his hand slides up underneath my nightie and he groans against my lips before finally breaking the kiss. My knickers are soaked.

"Someone's made a mess of her undies," he teases, slipping a finger inside the elastic. His callous finger brushes over my clit and I buck my hips up.

"Being pregnant makes me horny, Simba," I admit, feeling a blush colour my cheeks.

"You make me horny, Temptress," he taunts, grabbing my hand and guiding it down towards his hard dick.

He continues teasing me with his finger for a moment, before stopping and letting out a bellowing laugh as he rips the fabric and discards my knickers to the floor.

He inhales a deep breath, and exhaling he groans, "You're so wet, temptress. Can I taste you?"

I respond with a gasp and a nod, words failing me. Not even thirty seconds pass before he's moving over on the bed and diving between my legs as I spread them wide. My hips buck the moment his tongue laves over my clit. It's been awhile since Ashton had gone down on me and I'd forgotten how incredible it feels. Right now being pregnant the feeling is heightened, and the moment his tongue darts inside my pussy I can feel my climax building.

"Oh my gosh, Ashton!" I scream out, covering my mouth with my hand afterwards. He yanks it away, chuckling against my clit, causing vibrations to rumble through my pussy.

"I'm going to come, Ashton," I admit, seconds before I'm trembling with my orgasm rocking through me. Ashton laves up every last drop, sending aftershocks through me. When he finally comes up for air he leans over me with a hand on my stomach and kisses me sweetly.

"I love you, Tempany. I'm so sorry I ever doubted us."

"I forgive you, Ashton. I love you too. I'll never stop loving you."

"Good. I'll never stop loving you and these babies as well."

He stands up from the bed and grabs my hands, pulling me up with him. I stumble a little but Ashton doesn't let me fall. He takes my hand to lead me out of the room.

"Let's go home, Temptress," he says softly, but with a hint of excitement in his voice. I'm excited about our future together, with our growing family. I never should have pushed Ashton away, but it's water under the bridge now. Our future is all that matters.

CHAPTER EIGHTEEN

Tempany

I t's crazy that so many weeks have gone by since I found out about my pregnancy. I regret the stupid fight I had with Ashton, as missing out on having him at the first ultrasound hurt a lot. I've been really sick, and Ashton has been by my side as much as he can be.

He'd taken me away for a weekend mini holiday and we'd spent the entire time naked and making love. It was bittersweet, as I felt like my body looked hideous with the bloating, but Ashton assured me I'd never looked more beautiful than I do carrying his babies.

He's holding my hand now, leading me into the doctor's surgery for my twelve-week ultrasound.

It's a special one for several reasons, one, that Ashton is by my side and two, we're finding out the genders.

We're also excited to finally be able to tell our family.

I hadn't even told my dad or step mum when I'd stay ed there whilst Ashton and I had fought.

So far, only Lorena, Ariel and Zeke know. Ava probably does as well, because I doubt Zeke would've kept his mouth shut.

It doesn't matter; they'll know soon enough if today's ultrasound goes well.

Ashton is extremely excited, so much so he's squeezing my hand, and his knees are bouncing in anticipation whilst we're sitting in the waiting room.

I'm still scared, even though this is the furthest point I've gotten into a pregnancy the worry hasn't subsided.

I've stupidly—constantly—googled all the worst case scenarios of infant loss, and it's opened my eyes in negative ways.

But Ashton is always the comfort.

Glancing over at me, he smiles.

"It's going to be fine Temptress. You've gotten this far."

I don't get to respond due to my name being called by the obstetrician.

Standing together, Ashton follows me. I'm dragging him behind me, anxious to get this ultrasound over with—to put my mind at ease—knowing my babies are healthy and growing strong.

CHAPTER NINETEEN
Ezekiel

I don't get nervous. Like ever. I've always been a chill guy and gone with the flow, but right now my nerves are eating me alive. Having moved back to Lockgrove Bay from the city, I'd shacked up with Ava, my girlfriend of over four years, who is my best mate Ashton's little sister.

Our friends have started to get hitched, and it seemed like Ava has bouquet catching voodoo because every damn time we've been at a wedding she's caught the bouquet. I'm not opposed to getting married, because quite frankly I'd marry Ava yesterday, but her brother is sometimes still a right tosser about us being together, and even though I'm a show pony who loves attention heaped on me I don't want the whole big shebang of a wedding.

But I know my girl, and her love for pretty-*sexy*-dresses, and she wants that, the whole big white wedding with all our friends and family there. Just thinking about that and what I'm about to do has me breaking out in a cold sweat.

Ashton will probably slaughter me when he finds out, but I'd been good and asked her mum for permission which she gladly gave me. Even Mathias–her stepdad–who was more like a dad to her than her own had even been before the sick fucker offed himself in jail. Ava deserves a father who loves her, and Mathias has definitely stepped up for her. He even said he'd happily walk her down the aisle, so I need to suck it up and propose to my girl.

Right now, she's kneeling on the floor, setting up the teddy bear themed Christmas tree in the middle of our living room. Everything with us is teddy bears, for every anniversary or significant event in our lives I give Ava a teddy bear. I'm starting to regret that choice as every night when I get into bed I have to shove twenty damn teddy bears to the floor before I can pull back the covers. But it's our thing, has been since I gave her the first one at her sixteenth birthday and took her first kiss as mine.

Ava Castello is mine, my forever hopefully.

She stands up, not realising I'm behind her.

Clearing my throat, I drop to my knee and she turns around with a gasp to find me down on one knee holding up a Christmas teddy bear with an engagement ring tied to the bow around the neck.

Her hands are over her mouth, but her gasps of surprise still escape her lips when I start to speak.

"Ava, I've loved you from the first time I laid eyes on you, my firefly."

"Zeke..." she murmurs, shifting excitedly on the spot.

"You've always been mine...so please be mine forever Ava? Be my wife, firefly?"

She's shocked, and my heart is racing. I'm worried I've fucked up and left it too long. Worried that she's going to say 'no' and I'm going to be wiping my eyes with the teddy bear, instead of giving it to her.

"Zekey bear," she sobs softly, dropping her hands down by her sides. "Oh my god, a thousand times yes!"

I stand, taking the ring off of the bow. "Really, firefly? You wanna marry me?"

"Of course, Zekey bear. I love you."

"I love you too, firefly. So damn much," I tell her, sliding the ring onto her finger. She smiles wide, admiring the sapphire and diamond-encrusted engagement ring on her finger. It sparkles under the lights of the Christmas tree, and I know at that moment this is one hundred percent the right choice. Seeing my beautiful Ava wearing my grandma's engagement ring and knowing that she's my forever is causing my heart to race and my dick to stir.

"It's my grandma's ring. When I told mum I was proposing to you, she wanted you to have it, firefly."

"Aww, Zekey bear, that's so sweet. I love it... and you."

I don't respond but pull her into my arms and kiss her, dropping the teddy bear to the floor. She breaks the kiss, laughing.

"Poor Christmas teddy," she says, picking him up and putting him on the mantle. She gives the teddy a kiss and then turns back towards me with a cute pout on her lips.

"What're you thinking, Ava Darby?"

"About celebrating our engagement," she admits, taking my hand and dragging me towards the bedroom.

She falls against the bed, right in the middle on top of her teddy bear menagerie. And holding up that very first teddy bear I got her, she beckons me closer with a curled finger as she teases, "Fuck me Zekey bear. Right here whilst I hold this bear."

I groan, gulping down the lump in my throat. I love the cute and sweet but dirty side of my girl.

"Fuck Ava," I say raspy. "The images you're putting in my head right now."

"What Zekey bear?" she asks, smirking and holding the teddy bear right at her pussy in her lace nightie.

Stepping towards her, I shove the rest of the teddy bears aside and kiss Ava hard.

"Did you ever play with yourself whilst holding that bear after we kissed, Av's?"

She looks up at me, her lip between her teeth. Her cheeks colour and she admits, "Yes, Zekey bear."

"Fuck Ava, that's so dirty. Show me."

She slides a hand into her knickers, starting to stroke her clit and moaning. I watch eagerly, my dick hardening as her moans increase.

"I'm so close, Zekey bear," she informs me, her voice raspy.

"Yeah, make yourself come for me, firefly."

She pauses a moment, sliding her knickers down her legs to her knees. Her bare pussy is now on display. She spreads her legs a little wider before she slips a finger inside her glistening pussy. "Oh fuck!" she calls out, pumping the finger in and out and brushing her thumb over her clit.

"Come, Ava," I demand.

Obeying my request, she trembles, slowing her movements as her orgasm rushes through her body as she mumbles breathily, "Fuck, oh fuck, fuck."

Withdrawing her hand she holds it up to me, smirking when she asks, "Wanna taste, Zekey bear?"

"Do I ever, firefly," I taunt, climbing onto the bed and grabbing her hand to lick every finger clean. I then grab the knickers still around her knees and yank them off, throwing them onto the floor. Bending down I lick her pussy, lapping up the remnants of her orgasm, sending aftershocks through her body.

She tugs on my hair, forcing me to look up at her. "You need to fuck me, Ezekiel."

I love when she calls me by my full name. Ava is the only person in the entire damn universe who can get away with that honour. I chuckle, yanking my trackies and boxers down in one swift movement to free my throbbing hard dick. Without saying a word, I climb on top of my fiancé and slide inside her pussy. I'm home, we're one, and that's exactly how it's going to be forever.

CHAPTER TWENTY
Ashton

Zeke is over at mine again. We've been seeing a lot more of each other recently and I'm digging it. Like old times we're playing video games, having found a new love with *Monster Hunter*. Zeke is ten times better at it than me, but that's also because I've been a space cadet lately with Tem being pregnant and work kicking my butt.

Zeke pauses the game and questions me, "Everything go ok the other day?"

"Yeah, but Tem is still scared. I wanna fix it and make her worries go away."

"I don't think you can, Ash man. Just gotta be there for her."

"Did putting a ring on my sister's finger fuck

with your brain?" I ask, laughing because I swear it's not my best mate I'm talking to right now.

He shakes his head, chuckling. "Nah...I've always been full of great advice."

"Right, sure Ezekiel," I goad him. "When are you going to marry Av's?"

"Soon, dickhead," he jeers. "Let me get used to being engaged first."

"Ok," I reply, biting my lip.

"And you can't talk dufus...when are you and Tem getting married? You've been engaged for years, bro."

He's not wrong, but Tempany and I wanted to wait to get married until we were settled in jobs and our own home—until we were financially stable.

I smile at Ezekiel, liking hearing him say 'bro'. "I can't believe we will actually be brothers," I mumble and then add to answer his question, "Soon...like really soon. I think we need to bring up the wedding before she starts to show with the twins."

"You think Tem would be ok with that?" he asks me, concerned.

"Nah...yeah...might cheer her up. I get the feeling she's scared because of how I reacted when I found out."

He laughs, slapping me on the side of the head.

"No shit, dufus. That was low, but yeah lock your girl down. Show her you're one hundred percent committed to her."

"I will, bro. But it's up to Tem. I'd do anything for her."

"I know bro. I'd do the same for Av's," he assures me, nodding, and pressing play on the game again. We continue in silence, except for the sounds from the tv. I'm still not sure he's the right guy for my sister, but I have to trust him, and trust that he loves her.

CHAPTER TWENTY-ONE

Tempany

Ava and Dakota have come over to go wedding dress shopping with me. I haven't told them I'm pregnant and that Ashton and I have decided to postpone our wedding.

We're in the formal wear shop, looking through the dresses.

"What kinda dress do you want?" Ava asks me with a sweet smile.

"Something with straps and lacy," I reply, shifting further along the racks of dresses.

"That sounds so pretty, Tem," Dakota voices, giving me a smile.

I nod, asking her, "What's Aspen up to today?"

"Day out with daddy. He didn't have appointments at the clinic so he took the day off."

"That sounds great. Things been ok?" Ava asks her.

"Yeah, she's been a little bit sassy lately, but that's starting school."

"Yeah," I reply, pulling a lacy dress off the rack. "She's in Miss Kobe's class right?"

"Yeah, she seems like a great teacher. Asp really likes her."

"She's great, and that's good," I reply, yanking another dress out.

"Maybe you'll be teaching her next year, Tem," Ava says sweetly.

I gulp, shaking my head. "Probably not."

"Oh, why not?" Ava questions me, her eyes darting to an equally shocked Dakota.

"Because...I...um, won't be teaching next year."

"Oh," Ava gasps, touching my arm softly. "Why not sis?"

I love that she calls me sis. It never gets old hearing that. Ava has welcomed me into her family just as much as Ashton has and I can't wait to have it be official. But I need to tell them now. I'm honestly surprised Ava doesn't know, as I would've put money on Zeke telling her.

Gulping and looking down at my feet, I reply, "Because I'll be on maternity leave."

They both gape at me, and Ava shrieks excitedly, "Oh my god, Tem are you pregnant?"

"Yeah, I am," I reply, not able to hide my smile. "About four months along, so probably shouldn't be trying on dresses now."

"Yeah. Are you postponing the wedding?"

"Yes. Ashton didn't want to but I don't want to be a pregnant bride," I admit, adding with a laugh, "I already feel like an elephant and I'm going to be huge."

"Why? Are you having more than one?" Dakota asks, eyeing me with a knowing smile.

I nod. "Yeah, I'm having twins."

"Oh my gosh, Tem, that's amazing and so exciting," Dakota says, grinning.

"Yeah, I can't believe it," I confess.

"Is Ashton excited?" Ava asks.

"Yeah, he keeps doting on me. Will barely let me lift a finger," I reply with a soft laugh.

"That's super sweet," Dakota says. "Knox was the same when I was pregnant with Aspen."

"It's so annoying," I respond, again laughing as I take one last dress off the rack.

"Do you still want to try on some dresses?" Ava questions me, pulling out a sweetheart neckline, lace bodice dress with wide straps, and a pink ribbon around the waist. It's absolutely beautiful.

"That's so pretty Av's," I say, taking it from her and turning it around to look at the back. It has tiny buttons from the waist up to the middle of the back.

"Try it on, Tem," Ava suggests. "I'm sure you'll look beautiful in it."

Dakota affirms Ava's suggestion with a nod. Holding the four dresses in my arms I head into the change room, with the girls following me.

Hanging the dresses up on the hooks, I run my fingers over the fabric, sighing as I look down at my stomach. I'm starting to show and I really don't want to be a pregnant bride. Taking the dress I love with the pink ribbon off the hook I carefully unbutton it, and pool it in a heap on the floor whilst I undress. My mind wanders–back to before Ashton and I got together–when I catch a glimpse of myself in the mirror in my lacy knickers and bra. I can't help but think of when he barged in on me in the bathroom wearing the lace bodysuit I had under my dress for our parents' wedding. I was in love with Ashton then, and honestly never really thought of him as my stepbrother. I've always loved him since we were kids, and being together, loving each other and getting married, about to have our own kids is the way it should be.

Stepping into the dress, I lift the fabric up and over my hips. Pulling it up I slip my arms through the straps and admire myself in the mirror for a moment, holding the dress closed at the back. Turning to the curtain I peek my head out and call out to my sister, "Av's can you come help me with the buttons?"

Ava slides the curtain across, slipping in behind me when she says, "Sure Tem." Our eyes catch in the mirror and I drop my hand so she can do up the array of buttons. Smoothing the tulle skirt down, I smile even wider.

"Wow, Tem, it's stunning. You look so beautiful."

"You think so? Will Ashton like it?"

"He'll love it, Tem. He'd think you're stunning in anything, but this is your dress."

I can feel tears stinging my eyes, and Ava says, "Should we show Kota?"

"Yeah," I muse, gathering up the tulle as I turn around whilst Ava slides the curtain across and steps out with me following.

Dakota can't help but smile as well. "Gosh, Tempany, that is so beautiful. You look amazing."

"Thanks," I reply, sniffing back tears. The happy tears, because as I take another look in the mirror I know without a doubt that this is my wedding dress. It's the dress I'm going to marry Ashton in. The dress I'm going to become his wife in. And I couldn't be happier.

"Is this your dress, Tem?" Ava asks sweetly.

"Yeah, this is my dress," I affirm, smiling and turning around to hug her. "I love you, Ava. Thank you for being such a great stepsister."

She smiles at me. "I love you too, Tempany. And I'm your sister."

"That means the world to me," I admit, shuffling back towards the changing room.

"I always wanted a sister, and I'm so glad my brother is marrying you."

She quickly helps me undo the buttons and I change back into my clothes, ready to go home and tell Ashton I've found my dress. I was hesitant about even trying on dresses but I'm glad I did.

CHAPTER TWENTY-TWO

Ava

I'm over at Ash & Tem's with Zeke. We're all lazing around the pool. Well, us girls are on loungers whilst the boys are in the pool, splashing around like juveniles. Tempany is laughing at them, and I join in momentarily. I'm not feeling the best, my stomach in knots. I must look pale, because Tempany turns to me and asks, "Av's are you ok? You look really white."

I shrug her comment off with a scoff. "I'm fine. Just got a bit of a stomach ache."

"Oh, something you ate? Or is your period due?"

I shake my head, trying to think back to when I last had a period. My cycle has been erratic lately with dancing more. I've had to up the number of classes I'm teaching due to demand and even though I enjoy it, it's wreaking havoc on my body in a lot of ways. I've been tired, irritable, and my cycles come when they want to.

"I don't know Tem," I answer, glancing over at her. Her expression is definitely concerning.

I think for a moment, turning to look fully at her as I calculate the last time I had a period in my head. It seems like yesterday, but months ago at the same time. I've been a little bloated which has caused my leotard to be extra tight around the middle, but it still fits and that's all that matters.

Tem touches my knee, which is now bouncing with anxiety.

"You should go to the doctors," she suggests with a sigh.

"Yeah, maybe," I respond, slightly nodding and adding, "I'm sure it's nothing. I'm probably just tired from working extra hours at the studio."

She nods in response. I stand then, and the whole world around me spins with overwhelming sudden dizziness. I hear Tem's voice, but can't make out what she's saying as my vision disappears and I'm out, everything fading into blackness.

IT SEEMS LIKE LONGER THAN A FEW minutes when I open my eyes to find Zeke kneeling beside me on the pool lounger.

"Fuck, firefly, you scared me," he admits, his wet hair dripping water over me as he shakes his head.

"Sorry," I mumble. "What happened?"

"You stood up and fainted Av's. I thought you were going to fall into the damn pool."

"Oh, well I guess I'm lucky then," I reply, laughing halfheartedly when a rush of pain hits my stomach, causing me to clutch it tightly and groan.

"Are you ok, Av's?" Zeke asks, concern painting his face.

I shake my head. Zeke takes my hands and pulls me up into his arms. "Let's get you home, firefly," he says, his voice shaky. I can tell he's worried about me, but I'm sure I'll be fine. Most likely it's just my period coming and once it starts I'll be ok.

CHAPTER TWENTY-THREE
Ezekiel

The entire car ride home I'm on edge, worried Ava is about to chunder all over the dashboard. She's as pale as a ghost and clutching her stomach.

"You ok, firefly?" I ask, rubbing my hand up and down her thigh to comfort her.

"Yeah, I'm just feeling a bit crampy."

"We'll be home soon, and I can run you a bath."

"That would be nice," she says, smiling through her pain. "I love you, Zekey bear."

"I love you, too, firefly," I reply, pulling into our driveway and cutting the engine. I'm really worried about her, but I'm trying not to show it by keeping a straight face.

I rush to get out of the car and run around the

back to open Ava's door for her. She takes my hand and I help her out. Wrapping my arms around her I kick the door shut and she leans into my side as we head inside.

I lead her straight to the bathroom, and she sits down on the toilet lid whilst I start to run her bath. I swear she's even paler now, and I'm so scared. Her periods have been horrible in the past, but this seems worse than anything my girl has experienced before. It doesn't make any sense.

"You sure you're ok, firefly?" I ask worriedly.

"Yes, I just want to get in the bath to help with the pain."

"Ok, do you need help getting undressed?"

She nods, and I help her up, gripping her bikini bottoms and pushing them down to the floor. She kicks them aside and I reach around her back to untie her top. I'm all thumbs but eventually the knots undo and it falls to the floor. I take a moment to admire her tits, wishing I could take the pink buds into my mouth. That always makes my girl melt for me, but now is not the time.

Now she's naked, I help her into the hot bath and turn off the taps so she's not scolded. A shiver rushes through her body, and she wraps her arms around her waist.

"Av's I don't like seeing you this way. I think you should go to the doctor's." I touch the back of my hand to her forehead; she's clammy but not feverish.

Again she shakes her head. "I don't want to," she refuses. "I'll be fine once my period starts or the stomach bug passes."

She lets out a sigh, leaning back in the water. Her stomach rises out of the water, and I run my palm over her flesh at her belly button.

"You're a bit bloated, Av's."

"I know. It has to be my period coming. I haven't had it in a couple months."

"Have you still got cramps?"

"Yeah," she replies, nodding and rubbing her lower belly.

"Want me to finger you?" I question, adding with a smirk, "You know cause making you come always seems to help."

She smiles at me, giving me an answer without her words.

Knowing I have her consent, my hand dives under the water and she spreads her legs wide for me. The moment I touch her clit, she gasps, bucking her hips towards my hand. I know what she likes, so I start to rub her clit with gentle strokes of my finger.

"Feel good, firefly?" I ask, smirking at her.

"Yes, so good," she murmurs, giving me a sweet soft smile.

Still rubbing her clit I insert a finger into her pussy, drawing it in and out in a steady rhythm. Her hips rock, splashing water over the side of the bath. I couldn't care less about the mess she's making. Getting her off to ease her cramps is the only thing on my mind, and she's getting close. Her breath is raspy, steady pants showing that she's on the edge and ready to fall. Leaning forward I kiss her, and swallow her moan as she comes.

Breaking the kiss, her smile is wider. "I'm guessing that was good?" I tease.

"Yeah, thanks Zekey bear. I love it when you make me come."

"I love making you come, firefly. Are your cramps a little better?"

"A lot," she responds, wobbling a little as she stands to get out of the bath. I help by wrapping a towel around her body, enveloping her in it before I follow her to the bedroom to help her get dressed. I'm looking forward to a night snuggling with her in bed. I'll do anything to make my girl feel loved and cherished, especially when she's struggling with pain. Ava is my everything, and I truly hope it's just her period coming and not something worse.

CHAPTER TWENTY-FOUR

Ava

Even though it's been hours since I took the pregnancy test I'm now holding in my hands, I can't stop staring at it. The two pink lines show a blazing positive. I'm pregnant. And by this test, I'm probably weeks along. With my cycles though I honestly don't have a clue when it would've happened. Zeke and I are always careful when we have sex, which is a lot, but if we don't use condoms then he always pulls out.

I'm not stupid. I know that's not foolproof, but I also honestly didn't think I'd have much chance of getting pregnant with my crazy–albeit often absent–cycles.

I'm pacing the room now, waiting for Zeke to get home from work. I'd taken the day off, calling in sick for my classes which left me feeling uneasy. I hate letting my students down, but ever since that day when I fainted I've been vomiting every morning, and pretty much all throughout the day so working has been difficult and I finally treated myself to a day on the couch.

I'd only taken the test late morning, hours after my first pee of the day and breakfast when the box of five I'd ordered online arrived in the mail. I didn't want to be a part of local gossip by heading into the chemist or the supermarket to buy pregnancy tests.

I nearly jump out of my skin when I hear the door slam, telling me Zeke is home. Plodding out to the kitchen with my bare feet, I hold the test behind my back. Zeke is unpacking his backpack, unloading his travel cup and plastic container into the dishwasher when I step up behind.

"Hey, Zekey bear. I have something to show you."

He turns to face me, his eyes lighting up with intrigue.

"What's that you've got behind your back, firefly?"

He nods to my hands. Stretching out my arms I hold the pregnancy test up to him.

"Seriously Av's!? You're fucking kidding me, right?"

"No. Why would I joke about being pregnant, Ezekiel!?" I yell.

"Because, I don't know, fuck..." he bellows, not even looking at me as he freaks out, storming out of the kitchen and straight out the front door. I hear his car roar to life and screech as he reverses out of the driveway before tearing off down the street.

I burst into tears. That didn't go at all how I thought it would. I honestly thought he'd be happy, maybe even shed a tear of happiness. But instead he freaked out and left me alone.

I don't know how to feel now. I wasn't elated to find out I'm pregnant, but I was kinda happy, especially because there was always a possibility that it wasn't meant to be.

But Zeke had stolen that moment of happiness from me with his negative reaction to what should've been happy news for us both. We're engaged, and surely starting a family together is just the next step in our relationship. However, Zeke's reaction is bringing up so many anxious feelings about not only my being pregnant, but also if we're even on the same page for our relationship. Ezekiel Alessio is the only boy I've ever truly loved, and I want it all with him. All of it, marriage and a family, but maybe that's not what he wants.

Sighing, I try to shake the anxious thoughts away, and head to the bathroom to run a bath. I've been extra horny lately as well, which is also clearly pregnancy related and I'd also online ordered myself a waterproof rabbit vibrator, so I might as well treat myself to some orgasms with that in the tub. Who knows when Zeke will be home, and if he'll still want to be my fiancé when he does. If I have to be a single mother I will be. I don't want to be without Zeke, and I want to share this with him, but it's his choice.

CHAPTER TWENTY-FIVE

Ezekiel

Arriving at my best mate's house I bash on the door, probably a little too violently, but my heart is racing. I can't fathom Ava being pregnant. We've been so careful when we've fucked lately, and I can only think of a few times in the last six months when I've not used a condom. Fucking her bare feels so damn good, but the risk is not worth the reward. I always pull out before I nut completely, but I've come inside her a bit without realising before pulling out. And now I'm paying the price for that.

The door opens and Tempany is standing there, rubbing her very round belly. *Fuck, she's a damn whale. Ava could end up being the same.*

Tempany greets me with a smile. "Hey Zeke, what're you doing here?"

"I need to talk to Ash," I roar, my voice panicked.

"He's not home," Tem informs me, "He's at school for some team building thing for basketball."

"Oh, shit, right. What time will he be home?"

Tem shakes her head. "I'm not sure. If you need to talk to him urgently I'd consider going there."

"Thanks, Tem," I respond, scuffing my feet on the porch as I turn to walk away. She calls out to me, "Are you ok, Zeke?"

I yell back, "Yep, I'm fine."

But I'm not. Ava is fucking *pregnant*. I'm going to be a fucking dad. I'm not ready for that.

Tem closes the door and I tear off down the street, heading towards the school at breakneck speed. I'll probably end up with a speeding fine but I couldn't give a rat's arse. I need to talk to my best mate, right fucking now.

JUST AS TEM TOLD ME, ASHTON IS WITH HIS basketball team barking orders at them as they prance around the gym. It's odd as fuck, but I don't question it.

He nods at me when I approach. "Hey bro, what're you doing here?"

"I need to talk to you now, bro," I plead.

He shakes his head, and points towards his players on the court who're shooting goals. "I'm kinda busy, Zeke."

"I get that, bro, but I'm freaking out mega."

"Fine, but it better be serious or I'm crashing your gala practice next week."

I nod, and inhale a deep breath. He pulls me aside, closer to the bleachers. I take in another deep breath, and then blurt out, "Ava's pregnant."

His expression changes to anger, and he balls his fist. "Excuse me!? What the fuck Ezekiel? Are you shitting me? You knocked up my sister?"

Clearly Ashton is pissed off. I honestly thought he'd be over all the bullshit of being protective of his sister. I might have knocked his sister up, as he so crudely put it, but I also put a ring on her finger. I'm unquestionably in love with Ava.

"Yeah, she's pregnant, Ash, and when she told me I lost it and panicked."

He takes my hand, forcing my gaze to his. "Do you love her?"

"Of course I fucking do, dickhead."

"Then why are you freaking out?"

"I'm not ready, man. I can't be a dad," I respond with a shaky voice.

"We're never going to be ready, man. But you just have to suck it up and be there for the woman you love. You told me not to be an idiot, and I'm telling you to take your own advice."

"True." I sigh. "Are you pissed?"

"Kinda," he replies with a snigger. "But honestly, I know you love Av's. I have to trust that you'll protect her and the baby you're having together."

"Thanks, man, that means a lot."

He slaps me on the back. "Go home and apologise for being a dickhead, then celebrate your news. I'll see you tomorrow."

I nod, affirming his words as I leave the gym.

On the way home, I stop in at the store to grab a bunch of flowers and a tiny yellow baby onesie. Ava is still in the kitchen, sitting on the breakfast stool with a mug in her hands. She pouts at me when I walk in and I give her a kiss on the cheek.

Handing her the flowers and onesie, I come out with, "I'm so sorry for how I reacted this arvo, firefly. I love you, and I'm excited to go through this journey with you."

Her pout changes to a sweet smile and putting the flowers on the bench beside her, she jumps off the stool and hugs me tightly.

"Thank you, Zekey bear. I love you too, and

honestly I'm petrified of having a baby but with you by my side I'll get through it."

Pulling back from the hug, I kiss her forehead and take her hand. "Wanna celebrate having a baby by practicing how to make babies?"

She laughs, tugging on my arm to drag me to the bedroom. She doesn't speak, but I know my Ava and she's giving me consent to fuck her brains out without words. I'm looking forward to having months of bareback sex, and also the more I think about it, the more I'm looking forward to starting a family with the woman I love.

CHAPTER TWENTY-SIX

Tempany

Ava is currently sprawled over my couch, moaning in agony.

"Being pregnant sucks," she groans with a loud sigh, "Everything hurts."

"Yeah, try being pregnant with twins," I jeer, rubbing my swollen belly. "I feel like an elephant."

Again Ava groans. "I can't even think about getting as big as you. I'm already so bloated and my back is killing me."

I plop down in the single armchair, stretching my legs out in front of me.

Laughing, I comment, "I hate to break it to you, Av's, but that's only going to get worse. And also when the baby starts to press down on your bladder, you'll constantly be in the dunny."

She exhales. "Oh god, stop."

"It's the truth Av's. Being pregnant sucks, but you have to think of the blessing of meeting your child at the end."

"I know, but that seems like so long away, and I don't know if I'm ready to be a mum."

I smile. "Don't stress yourself out with worry. I think you'll be a great mum."

She sits up, stretching her arms over her head and yawning.

"You'll be a great mum, Tem. Ashton is so excited to be a dad as well."

Again I rub my belly, causing the twins to kick visibly. Ava's eyes light up at the sight.

"Wow! Are they kicking again?"

"Yeah, they're active little ones, especially at this time of the day."

Ava laughs. "Yeah, they're like 'mum, it's dinner time.'"

"Yep," I reply with a nod and chuckle.

"Can I feel it?" Ava asks, reaching out towards me tentatively.

"Of course you can, Av's. Honestly, you of all people don't have to ask me that."

She rubs my belly, her palm grazing over my belly button and right on cue the twins kick again. Seeing their four feet pressing against my skin is so amazing, and quite frankly tickles. The sensation causes me to laugh and hiccup at the same time.

Ava laughs as well, and then says, "Stop Tem, if you keep laughing I'll end up with the hiccups and then I'll vomit."

I inhale a deep breath to calm myself. "Have you had a lot of morning sickness?"

Ava laughs hysterically. "A lot, like heaps," she complains. "I've been so sick I can barely keep water down, but I'm also so insanely thirsty, it's crazy."

"Maybe you're having twins as well," I joke, holding my hands up in a questioning pose.

"Oh god, I hope not!" Ava shrieks, visibly swallowing hard as though she's swallowing down a large lump in her throat.

She stands from the couch, swaying a little from side to side as though she's dizzy. I stand as well, grabbing her hands to steady her. "Careful, Av's. Dizziness is a big symptom too."

"I know. I've been really dizzy too, but it will pass in a minute."

"Will you be ok to drive home?"

"Yeah, it's only a short drive," she replies, heading towards the door. I follow her out and hug her goodbye, which is a little awkward with my large belly.

I'd put money on Ava also having twins, but

I'm not one to gamble, and we'll find out soon enough when she has her eight week ultrasound. It would be uncanny if both of the Castello siblings had twins. People would start thinking there's something in the water of Lockgrove Bay.

CHAPTER TWENTY-SEVEN
Ava

Waddling down the hospital hallway, I try not to inhale the overpowering smell of bleach permeating the space.

I've been insanely unwell the past few weeks with my pregnancy and can't believe I'm not even eight weeks along yet.

We've booked an ultrasound for just after I hit eight weeks and I'm absolutely petrified, especially with Tem putting the idea in my head of having twins. I'm not totally against the idea of more than one kid, but having them at the same time seems scary and utterly overwhelming. I'm exhausted now–violently ill near twenty-four seven–and I just can't fathom the new mum's tiredness times two.

I turn to look at Tem who's walking beside

me–waddling even more so than me–and ask, "Do you know what room she's in?"

"Yeah, room seven, up the end of the hallway."

I glance at the numbers on the door, noting we've just gone past room five. I don't like being in the hospital, and I'm thankful I've never had to experience being in one in my life. I've not even broken a bone, even with dancing my whole life. Now, the only times I've been in a hospital is when friends and family members have had babies and when Dakota had her accident a few back. I'd thought I was going to lose my best friend, but thank the heavens above she pulled through and now has Knox as her husband and their daughter Aspen.

She's such a sweetheart and I hope I have a daughter so they can become besties too.

It seems like an endless hallway when we finally get to Ariel's room. Tempany knocks and Ariel's voice grunts out, "Come in."

Opening the door we find Ariel sitting up in bed, cradling her baby boy in her arms. Well, not her baby boy, but Briston and Jebediah's baby boy. Ariel's selfless choice to be a surrogate for her best friend and his husband is truly amazing. I'm not selfish–by any means–but I couldn't imagine going through a pregnancy and becoming attached to the child and then having to give them up. At least though with Ariel's situation she'll still get to be a part of the child's life, as an auntie.

"Hey, Ar's. How're you doing?"

She chuckles softly. "I'm ok, but this little guy is having a bit of trouble with attachment."

I step closer to the bed, and look down at the baby. He's utterly perfect, and looks exactly like Jeb. "Aww, that's ok. He'll get it," I reply, smiling.

"Yeah, Bris and Jeb want him to be breastfed as much as possible."

I glance at Tem, standing on the other side of the bed. "That's great, Ariel," she responds. "They want their son to have the best start in life."

"Yeah, I'd do anything for Bris, so what he wants is what he'll get," she replies with a laugh.

"What's his name?" I ask, brushing a tiny strand of hair off his forehead.

"Isaiah Lucas."

"That's a unique name," I respond. "Are they choosing a last name?"

Ariel shakes her head, replying, "No, they're hyphenating, so his full name is Isaiah Lucas Nicholls-Harriss."

"A little bit of a mouthful, but it's still sweet," Tempany comments.

"Yeah, Briston insisted on both his having a middle name and the hyphenation. I couldn't say no."

Shifting in the bed, Ariel moves to put Isaiah into the plastic crib by the bed. He doesn't make a fuss, just kicks his little feet a few times before he settles.

Ariel sighs. I can tell something is up, other than just the new baby blues getting her down.

"You sure you're ok, Ar's?"

She nods and shakes her head at the same time, laughing. "To be honest, I'm ok, but I'm not."

"Why? What's going on?" Tempany asks.

"Yeah, can we help?"

"It's just hard at the moment on my own with the kids. I'm missing Brae so much, whilst he's on tour."

"Oh wow, yeah, that must be tough," Tempany supplies.

I add, "Where's Bria and Kyler now?"

"Staying with Bris and Jeb, and most likely causing havoc like they always do when they stay with uncle Bris."

"Sounds like he'll be a great dad," I comment laughing.

"Yeah, he will be," Ariel responds, nodding and looking over at Isaiah in the crib. She exhales a loud yawn, which is our cue to leave.

"We should be going,"Tempany offers. "We'll leave you to get some rest, and let me or Av's know if you need anything when you get out of the hospital."

"Thanks, but Brae will be back on Thursday to pick me up."

"I bet you're looking forward to seeing him," I tease, winking.

"Yeah, the kids are having a couple extra nights with Uncle Bris so Brae and I can have some alone time," she tells us. "Not that I'll be able to do anything, but even just kissing him will be nice."

"Yeah," I reply, laughing as we start to walk out of the room, "Bye Ariel."

"Bye, Av's, Bye Tem," she replies, her eyes already drifting shut as Tem closes the door behind us.

We don't talk on the way back to my house. There aren't any words to say. We're both exhausted and when Tem drops me home, I wave goodbye, go inside, and collapse on the bed. It's not long before I fall into a dreamless sleep.

CHAPTER TWENTY-EIGHT
Ezekiel

Going to the ultrasound makes Ava's pregnancy real. She's actually having my baby and I'm going to be a dad. *A dad.*

I'm not going to be able to send this child home to their parents when they're a little shit at school. They'll send the kid home to me and I'll have to deal with the consequences. I'm scared, terrified that my child will be a carbon copy of me and be an absolute little shit. I was a devil at school, spending most of my days in the principal's office or in detention. I'm honestly surprised I even passed school and Uni to become a music teacher. Pure fluke and other smarts if you ask me.

I can't worry about that now though, as I need

to be present for Ava. She's clutching my hand in a death grip. I've hated seeing her so unwell these past few weeks since we found out. It truly breaks my heart to see her in pain.

Her name is called and I help her stand up from the waiting room chair–hands on her shoulders a moment–to steady her as a wave of dizziness hits her.

Not only has she been nauseous and vomiting near nonstop, but she's been dizzy. She's had to take some time off from teaching her dance classes and that is taking a toll on her. She loves teaching dance–it's her dream career–and she's amazing at it. Watching Ava dance–and teach–is mesmerising. My girl is stunning, and I know her body will change during pregnancy and after she has the baby, but honestly that doesn't matter to me. Ava Castello–soon to be Ava Alessio–will always be the most beautiful woman in the world to me. I thought otherwise when I found out she was pregnant, but that was just my fear of the unknown getting to me.

Following the ultrasound technician into the room I can tell Ava's nervous. I am too, but I'm trying to hide it from her. I don't want to increase her anxiety and from how unwell she's been I'm ninety percent sure everything's okay with the baby. The technician asks Ava to lie down on the exam table. I sit on the swivel stool on the opposite side of the bed to the ultrasound machine.

The technician smiles and says, "Hi Ava and dad, are you ready to see your baby?"

"Yes," Ava rasps, smiling. I nod in response and squeeze Ava's hand.

"Great," the technician responds, "You're about eight weeks along, correct?"

"Yes, I think so," Ava replies. "I have PCOS and I'm a dancer so my periods are often irregular."

"That's fine, we'll get a better idea once we see your baby."

"Ok," Ava responds, gasping when her t-shirt is lifted up and the cold gel is applied to her belly.

"It's cold," she hisses.

"Sorry about that. It won't take too long and I'll be able to print some images for you to take home."

The technician glides the wand over Ava's belly and blurry images appear on the screen. It just looks like blobs and grainy black and white lines.

The technician gasps, and the colour drains from Ava's face. My stomach sinks.

"Is something wrong with the baby?" Ava asks, her voice shaky.

"No, not at all," the technician replies with a

slight smile, moving the wand around so the blobs on the screen expand and are a little clearer. "You're not having one baby, Ava. You're pregnant with twins!"

"Twins!" I exclaim, feeling my stomach flip flop with anxiety.

"Oh my gosh, really?" Ava questions, staring at the screen as the technician points at the two areas on the screen not full of blobs or lines.

"Yes, this is baby one," she says, showing us a tiny blob in one circle, "and this here is baby two."

"Wow, I'm having twins," Ava says, her voice trembling. She looks towards me, tears in her eyes. "Zekey bear, we're having twins."

"Yeah, firefly, two babies," I respond with a hint of anxious laughter.

"Can we find out the genders?"

The technician shakes her head.

"Not yet, maybe at your next appointment, closer to twelve weeks."

She wipes over Ava's belly with a wet wipe and pulls her t-shirt down again.

"So how many weeks along am I?" Ava asks, sitting up on the exam bed.

"I'd say about nine weeks, so we'll book you in for a twelve week scan and we'll hopefully be able to find out the genders then, but it can be tricky with twins."

"Ok, thank you. Are the babies ok?"

The technician nods in response to my question. "Of course, they're both measuring both on target."

"That's great, thanks."

"I'll just go grab the images for you. You might want to share with your family but it is still early, so be mindful."

Ava nods and I squeeze her hand as I help her up off the exam bed.

"Damn, firefly, we're having twins! Are you ready for two babies?"

"Not really, but it explains the sickness. And we'll be ok. We're in it together, Zekey bear."

I smile at her as we leave the room, and reply, "That we are, Ava."

We collect our ultrasound images and book in the next scan at the reception desk before leaving. We're having family dinner at the Castello's tonight and I can't wait to share our news with them. I just hope nothing goes wrong before our twelve week scan. Ashton and Tempany have gone through that and I can only imagine that kinda pain. My heart couldn't handle it.

WE'RE SITTING AROUND THE CASTELLO'S giant dining room table about to gorge on the delicious roast lamb feast Sasha has served up. These monthly family dinners have become a regular thing, Ashton here with Tempany and me with Ava. I'm glad Fidel is out of their lives though. He was never fit to be a father and Mathias, their stepfather, has really stepped up and given my best mate and my girl the father they deserve.

Ava must actually be feeling hungry since she piles her plate high with food, and covers it in gravy.

"Seriously, Av's, leave some for the rest of us," Ashton chastises.

She scoffs at him. "I'm really hungry, Ashy. And I can't resist mum's lamb roast."

We've not mentioned anything to their parents yet about Ava being pregnant. Only Ash and Tem know, so it isn't really his place to say anything, but still he blurts out, "Anyone would know you're pregnant, Ava."

That fucking does it.

Ava bursts into tears and Ashton hangs his head, mumbling, "Sorry, Av's. I didn't mean to blurt it out."

"Not cool, bro. It was our news to share."

"I'm sorry bro," Ashton apologises, looking

towards Sasha whose eyes are bugging and glancing every which way between us.

She focuses on Ava. "Ava, honey, is it true?"

Ava looks up at her mum, sniffing back tears when she replies, "Yes, mum, I'm pregnant with twins."

Sasha's face beams wide with a grin. "Oh sweetie, congratulations," she exclaims, her voice almost breaking with happiness, "And to you as well, Ezekiel."

"Thank you, mum. After the initial shock, we're very excited."

"Twins must run in your family," Mathias comments with a hint of laughter.

"Yeah, you're probably getting all your grand-children at once," I comment, picking up a forkful of roast lamb.

"Yes, and I'm so beyond grateful for you all. We're all so lucky to have love and children in our lives."

We nod in agreement and hoe into our food. Sasha Castello sure knows how to cook. Ava got some of the cooking gene, but we resort to pre-prepared things most of the time because we're tired and time poor. That's certainly not going to change with two babies to care for, but I'm ready for it all.

Family means the world to me. All I can hope

for now is that Dane comes home. I've not even been able to speak to him lately as the connection has been shitty on their base. Having your brother fighting a never-ending war overseas–not even knowing exactly where he is located–is torturous. I want him home. I want him to be able to meet his nieces or nephews. But I'm scared of who he's become. I don't know if he'll be the brother I remember. All I can do is hope for the best with his return and the birth of my babies.

Hope is all we have.

CHAPTER TWENTY-NINE

Ashton

Tempany wakes with a start, screaming, "Ashton! Oh my god, I think my water broke!"

Blinking furiously, I try to get my bleary eyes to focus on the clock beside the bed. It's blurry, but I can just make out the numbers.

2:05am.

I yank back the covers as Tem sits up. The bed is saturated.

"Oh shit, Tem. Do we need to go to the hospital, like now?"

She shakes her head. "I don't think so. The contractions are only just starting."

"Ok, tell me if they get worse. I'll go get your bag and stuff ready." I leap out of bed, trying not to give Tem any indication of how anxious I am.

The reality is hitting me–that in mere hours–I'm going to be a dad. A dad to twins. The thought is overwhelming and exciting.

Tempany has started taking deep breaths in, focusing on her breathing like the midwives showed us.

I'm in the laundry–grabbing out some clean sheets–when I hear Tempany scream out in agony. I rush back into the bedroom, throwing the sheets on the floor as I rush to her side.

"Are you ok, Tem?" I question, knowing it's probably a stupid question to be asking when it's clear she's far from ok.

"The...contractions...are...getting...closer," she huffs out, breathing deeply between each word.

I sit on the edge of the bed and take her hands in mine.

"Did you want to leave for the hospital now?" I ask, my voice shaky. My heart is beating erratically because I'm so scared for her.

She nods, huffing out a shaky breath when she replies, "Yeah. It hurts so much, Simba."

Still holding her hands I stand from the bed, and help her up. She stumbles and grabs her stomach as a contraction hits. Seeing her in pain is heartbreaking.

"Breathe, Tem, in...out," I encourage. She glares at me, and I bite my lip. I won't say anymore. Pain makes her grumpy, and I can tell this pain is next level.

I lead her out of the bedroom–grabbing her hospital bag from by the door–and take her to the car. I open the car door and help her get in. She groans from her whole body aching and the awkwardness of getting into the car, and then sighs as she sits back in the seat and I close the door.

After getting into the car myself, I drive as fast as I can without breaking the law *too* much.

By the time we arrive at the hospital, Tempany's contractions are coming fast with barely a minute between them. These babies are coming *now*.

I pull up outside emergency, and rush inside to get a wheelchair. I help Tem get into it and push her inside, not caring that I've left the car parked in the hospital driveway. There are more important things to worry about right now.

The nurse looks straight at us, chuckling a little when she says, "Looks like someone is ready to have a baby."

"Yes! Get these babies out of me now!" Tempany bellows, gripping the side of the wheelchair as a contraction hits her.

"Oh, babies," the nurse says with a chipper tone. "Who's delivering them?"

"Doctor Findley is our doctor and Alice is our midwife," I inform the nurse.

"I'll page them both now. Head through to the maternity ward."

I glance up at the overhead signs, easily locating the maternity ward to the left of us. I push the wheelchair down the corridor, focusing on breathing to calm myself whilst Tempany screams down the walls.

We don't even make it to the maternity ward waiting room before Alice finds us.

"Hello, you two. Seems as though your babies are ready to enter the world."

"Most definitely," I reply as she shows us into a delivery room. "Is Doctor Findley available?"

"No, he's not on call tonight, so it will just be me delivering for you, unless we have any complications."

Tempany gasps hearing the word 'complications'. I don't blame her for that reaction. It must be even scarier for her than me right now.

Once in the delivery room, Alice helps Tempany up onto the bed and hooks up the machines to her to monitor the babies heartbeats. She then gets her to spread her legs, and pulls her soiled underwear down. Tempany shifts uncomfortably as Alice checks her dilation.

"Well, Tempany, I have some good news for you."

"What's that?" Tem stammers, breathing through another contraction.

"You're fully dilated, and your babies are ready to arrive."

"Wow, Tem, we're going to meet our babies," I exclaim, excited.

Tempany doesn't respond, instead she just hisses through another contraction and nods.

"Are you ready to push, Tempany?" Alice asks. Again Tempany just nods, and Alice stands at the end of the bed. "Ok, with the next contraction, I want you to bear down and push like you're going to the toilet."

Alice only just gets the words out when Tempany follows through, pushing through her contraction. "Great work, Tempany. Keep going."

Once more, Tempany pushes through her next contraction, and then a third time before she screams, "God, it hurts!"

"You're doing great," Alice reassures her, "one more push and we might see your first baby."

Tempany pushes again, sweat beginning to pour down her forehead, slicking her long blonde hair to her forehead. I step up beside the bed and take her hand. She squeezes it like a vice when she pushes, and Alice exclaims, "I can see baby one's head. Push Tempany!"

It's barely a minute after the fourth push that we hear the cries of a baby. "Congrats, baby one is a boy!"

Tempany gives me a smile.

"Our boy, Tem."

I'm elated. Glad that at least one of the genders predicted at our ultrasounds was correct. You can never be too sure with these things.

"Ok, Tempany, just a few more pushes and baby number two will be with us."

Alice is right. Tempany only pushes hard twice before our second baby arrives with an even louder cry. "And baby number two is a girl."

Tempany sighs, and starts to sob.

"Ashton, would you like to cut the cords?"

I look at Tempany and she nods. I take the scissors from Alice and cut the cords. She scoops our babies up, and quickly cleans off the vernix coating their pale skin before she brings them back over to Tempany. She places them side by side on Tempany's chest and Tempany kisses both their foreheads in turn. Alice unhooks the machines and cleans up the room before she says, "I'll leave you both for a while to get to know your babies. Press the call button if you need me."

"Thank you, Alice," I reply, pulling a chair up beside the bed.

Tempany is grinning. "They're so beautiful, Ashton."

"I know, Tem. Are you certain of the names yet?"

She nods, her grin growing even wider when she says, "Yes. Ander Jude and Aliah Jules."

"Beautiful, Tempany. Suits them perfectly."

We sit in silence then, admiring our babies. I've never felt more love than I did at that moment. Love for Tempany, and love for my babies. We never thought we'd get to this point, and I'm beyond happy. Alice comes back in to continue cleaning up, checking to make sure Tempany had passed the placenta. She gets cribs for the babies, and name cards. I help Tempany have a shower, before calling our family to tell them the good news. Our babies made a very quick entrance to the world, but all is well.

CHAPTER THIRTY
Tempany

It has been a crazy whirlwind six weeks since the twins made their dramatic, middle of the night entrance into the world. I'd barely had time to think, let alone care for myself since their arrival. It has been constant pumping, then feeding, running on no sleep on repeat. I can't even remember showering much since Ashton went back to work after his two weeks father's leave. I'd decided to not go back to school until the twins go to kindy. I want to spend as much time with them as I can when they're little.

I'm an absolute mess right now, still in my pj's that are covered in baby vomit and spit up and smell absolutely rotten. I'm surprised that Lorena, who is over with her two kids Grady and Lucy, after school can stand being around me without chundering herself. I adore her kids and she's been an absolute godsend answering all my baby questions and she's been a listening ear when I've called in the middle of the night crying because I'm so overwhelmed with having twins.

I'm so grateful for her.

She follows me into the kitchen and I flick the kettle on, before telling her, "Help yourself to a coffee, Lo. I'm just going to have a shower."

She smiles, giving me a wink and replies, "No worries. Take your time and enjoy it."

I head to the ensuite bathroom, and strip off. I stare at myself in the mirror for a moment, and sigh. My stomach is still quite round, the skin also hasn't bounced back either. I know it's only been six weeks and I had twins but I feel like my body will never be normal again. My boobs still haven't gone down in size either, but considering I'm still pumping milk up to ten times a day that's not at all surprising. Ashton hasn't made any comments about my body, but I still feel self conscious and I'm hoping I'll still look nice in my wedding dress in a couple months time. I was cautious about postponing our wedding until the twins were born, but I know I wouldn't have felt comfortable getting married when I was the size of an elephant.

Turning the water on, I tap my foot waiting for

it to heat up and when it's warm I step under the showerhead. Tipping my head back I let the water flow over my hair and down my back. It feels divine.

The best shower I've ever had. After thoroughly wetting my hair, I squeeze out a palm full of shampoo. It's probably overkill, but my hair is so dirty I'm surprised it's not insanely itchy.

I lather up and massage the foam into my scalp. It feels so good.

I rinse out the shampoo and then slather the ends in conditioner, letting that soak in whilst I wash the rest of my body with my caramel body wash.

After washing the conditioner out, I get out of the shower and wrap myself in the big fluffy towels from the heated towel rack Ashton decided to install on a whim whilst I was pregnant. I thought it was a stupid idea–an unnecessary item– but now I love it. It serves the dual purpose of helping the towels dry and making them fluffy so they feel nice against your skin after a shower.

Heading in the bedroom I dry off and check my phone which is charging on the bedside table. There's a message from Ashton.

> Be ready when I get home, temptress. I'm taking you out for the night.

I smile widely and reply:

> ok Simba ☺

I DECIDE TO PUT ON SOME SEXY LACY underwear and a maxi length jersey fabric black dress, with thin straps and a deep v neck line that shows off my cleavage.

After dressing, I head into the kitchen unable to wipe the smile from my face. Lorena notices my change in disposition.

"You seem happier, Te."

"Yes, I feel so much better."

"You look great!" Lorena beams. "Why the nice dress?"

"Ashton is taking me out on a date night. Are you able to stay and look after the twins?"

"Of course, I'll just call Beau and get him to pick up my two on his way home from work."

"Are you sure? I can call Ava or Dakota if that's easier."

"It's fine, I miss being around babies."

"Ok thanks," I respond with a smile, flitting back out of the kitchen to go back to the bathroom to dry and curl my hair.

WHEN ASHTON ARRIVES HOME AN HOUR later, Beau is also just arriving to pick up Grady and Lucy. They exchange pleasantries and Ashton comes inside and kisses me on the cheek.

"You look beautiful, temptress."

"Thanks, Simba."

"Just give me ten minutes to shower and change and we can head out."

"Ok, I'll just sort things out with Lo for the twins."

Lorena is sitting on the couch, and the twins are in their lounge room portable crib.

"Are you sure you'll be ok with everything, Lo?" I ask timidly, worry lacing my voice.

"Of course. I know you've got milk in the fridge ready to go, and I can use a baby bottle. Everything will be fine. Just go and enjoy your date night."

Ashton comes out, all dressed in dark black jeans, a grey and white striped shirt, and a black leather jacket. He looks gorgeous.

"Damn, Simba, you scrub up nice," I tease.

"So do you, temptress. That dress is stunning, but you might need a jacket. It's getting chilly outside."

"Ok, I'll grab my black cardigan on the way out."

He takes my hand, and leads me to the door. I grab my cardigan off the coat rack, and call out to Lorena, "See you when we get home, Lo."

"No worries, Te. Have a good time," she calls back as Ashton closes the door behind us and leads me to his mustang.

He helps me get in the car, before getting in himself and I feel a bit giddy. This feels like old times and my heart is thrumming in anticipation of the night ahead.

CHAPTER THIRTY-ONE

Ashton

I'd been planning this date night for weeks, trying to think of the perfect date for Tem. With the twins now in our lives we'd not had much time to ourselves, and I knew I had to bite the bullet to spend some time with the woman I love. She'd told me Lorena was coming over for a coffee this afternoon, so it was the perfect opportunity to make this date happen.

She's grinning as I drive, asking me, "Where are we going, Simba?"

I chuckle with my reply, "You'll find out when we get there." I'm teasing her, but she must have some idea of where we're heading as I indicate to turn onto the esplanade. It's the only road that leads to the basketball court and main beach.

Pulling up in the carpark, I cut the engine

and get out of the car. Tempany hesitates but gets out, whilst I grab a basketball out of the boot.

"Ready for a game of one on one, temptress?" I taunt, bouncing the ball in front of me and walking backwards towards the court.

"Oh, you're on, Simba," she taunts back, leaning in and smacking the ball out of my grip. She bounces it effortlessly, practically skipping up to the ring, and shooting for a goal. She nails it, the ball skimming the rim before it falls through the basket.

"Damn, temptress, you've been practicing."

She laughs, bouncing the ball around me in a ring. "Yeah, nah, I'm just a natural. Been playing since I was six you know."

"Oh I know, temptress," I goad, stealing the ball from her this time and going for a slam dunk, which I sink. I've still got it.

Tempany laughs, and scoffs, "Show off!"

"You love me!"

"Yeah I do," Tempany replies, giving me a playful slap on the butt. "So is this our entire date? I'm sure you didn't dress up nicely for a game of basketball."

"It's not the entire date," I tell her, tucking the ball under my arm and heading back towards the car.

I open the boot and throw the ball back in. "We're leaving?" Tempany questions.

"No, we're not leaving," I tell her, grabbing out the rolled up picnic blanket and basket of goodies I'd picked up from Melba's before heading home to pick her up.

"Wow, Ashton, that looks delicious," she expresses, licking her lips.

I tuck the blanket under my arm, hook the basket in the crook of my elbow, and slam the boot down with my other hand before I take Tempany's hand to head down to the beach. "Yeah, I know. I heard about Melba's making pre-made picnic baskets and thought a date night would be a great way to try them."

Reaching the beach, I drop the basket down on the sand and smooth out the blanket. Tempany sits down, folding her legs underneath her. I plop down beside her and unload the basket. There's ham and pickle sandwiches, chocolate coated strawberries, pretzels, and dip. Everything looks delicious, and handing Tem a sandwich we eat in silence, staring at each other. I'm honestly the luckiest guy in the damn world. Tempany is utterly stunning, and she loves me. She chose me. I'd been such a fool with denying myself for so long with her, but our love story is romance novel worthy.

After finishing the sandwiches I tease Tempany with the chocolate coated strawberries, rubbing it over my lips and biting into it with a moan before I put it between her lips. She moans as she bites into it.

I laugh and we both eat them until there's none left.

"I think we should save the pretzels and dip for later," I suggest.

"Yeah, I think that's a good idea."

I put them back in the basket and set it aside, leaning into Tem's side a little more.

She smiles at me, asking, "What're you thinking about, Simba?"

I exhale. "Just that this is where I first fell in love with you, temptress. I was so in denial about my feelings for you, but look where we are now. In love, with newborn twins and finally about to have the wedding we've dreamt of."

"Aww Ashton," she coos, "I love you so much, and I can't wait to marry you."

I kiss her then, hard because there are no words to answer. I've missed her so much. We've barely touched, let alone kissed since the twins were born. Gripping her waist, I gently push her down onto the blanket. I continue kissing her, exploring her mouth with my tongue whilst we pash like teenagers. She giggles into the kiss, and I break it and look down at her.

"What's so funny temptress?"

"Do you remember that time we came to the beach with Ava and you wouldn't stop staring at me in my black bikini?"

"Yeah, I remember," I reply, smiling because I remember exactly what I was thinking about that day and it was a lot more than kissing her.

"What were you thinking about that day?"

"Kissing you," I admit, kissing her softly, before adding teasingly, "and fucking you."

"Of course," Tempany responds, laughing.

I poke her in the side, asking, "Is it ok to have sex yet?"

She nods, a big smile on her face that causes my dick to stir in my jeans. "Yeah, it's been over six weeks. The doctor gave me the all clear."

I smirk, sitting up and jumping to my feet to pack up the picnic stuff. Tempany stands up and awkwardly holding everything, we sprint back to the car. It's been way too long since we've had sex and I have to tell Ash Jnr to calm himself down or we aren't even going to make it back to the car, let alone home, before I'm making love to Tempany.

BY THE TIME WE GET HOME, I'M SO ON EDGE and horny I want to take her in the driveway.

We head inside and Lorena barely has time to shrug on her jacket before I'm rushing her out the door. Tempany catches my gaze and laughs, soft and knowing, like she's just as on edge as I am. For her it's probably even more so, since Tempany is not one to take care of her own needs like I would.

When the door closes behind Lorena, the house is quiet in what is now a rare way that is few and far between now. No crying. No chaos. Just us.

Six weeks isn't long, but it's long enough to wonder if things will feel the same. I'm not honestly doubting it will, but Tempany has pushed two babies out, so you never know. I don't care though. She's still my temptress.

Stepping closer, resting my forehead against hers, I ask, "You okay, temptress?"

She nods, her hands finding my waist and fumbling with my belt. "Yeah, Simba. I've just... missed you."

I kiss her gently at first. Her lips are warm, and she sighs into my mouth. It's a kiss that shows how strong our connection is.

"I love you, temptress," I murmur against her lips, just breaking the kiss.

She smiles, eyes shining. "I love you too, Simba."

"Are you sure it's ok to have sex?"

"Yeah, please, Ashton, I need you now," she pleads, taking my hand and dragging me to our bedroom.

Once through the door, I'm kissing her again, harder this time. Stumbling towards the bed we start to discard our clothes, dropping them in a trail. Tempany is now naked, stopping right at the end of the bed. I step back, taking a moment to admire her body.

Smirking, I remark, "Wow, temptress."

She blushes. "What? Am I hideous?"

"Far from it, Tem. You're even more beautiful."

She moans and dives toward me, kissing me breathless. I still have my boxers on and hooking her fingers in the waistband, she pushes them down to the floor and palms my dick. Her touch causes me to groan as I push her down on the bed. The tip of my dick brushes over her clit, causing her to break the kiss and moan, "Please, Ashton, please fuck me now."

I don't have to be asked twice, sliding inside her insanely wet pussy. She's so turned on, so I slip in easily, and start to thrust. Leaning over her body, as I thrust in and out, I kiss her softly. She shifts beneath me, her hips bucking to meet my thrusts. It feels so good, so right, perfect. Breaking the kiss, Tempany moans, "Feels so good, Ashton."

"Yeah, Tempany. I'm going to come so hard and deep inside your pussy."

As though my words are a switch, with another deep thrust I feel Tempany shiver, her body trembling as her climax hits. I follow, falling against her chest as I unload inside her, my dick pulsing and filling her with cum.

Pulling out, I collapse on the bed beside her, spent but satisfied.

"That was great, Simba," Tempany says, tilting her head to look at me.

"It's always great with you, temptress," I reply, turning my head to kiss her.

Shifting up the bed, Tempany settles in my arms. We let the quiet wash over us, focusing on our breathing and embracing the calm of the afterglow. All that matters is the person next to me. My temptress, my whole world.

She breathes softly against my shoulder, her breath warm, steady and calm. I can feel every rise and fall of her chest, as she snuggles closer to me. I love these moments, cuddling skin to skin. It feels even more intimate than having sex. I trace lazy patterns on her back, calming her more and enjoying having her close.

I think about the twins, curled up in the next

room in their cots, asleep. An overwhelming feeling of gratitude hits me. Every moment, even the ones that were difficult and painful to bear have brought us here.

I glance at Tempany beside me and can't help but smile. She looks so tired but happy. My mind wanders to all the things we've been through to get here—the miscarriages, moving back to Lockgrove Bay, and then the birth of the twins and the sleepless nights, hard choices, the times we almost gave up on trusting each other—and I realise how much stronger our love has become. How much closer we've become.

"I love this," I murmur, mostly to myself, but she hears me and smiles, squeezing my hand. "This," I clarify, "All of it. This life. This quiet, after everything."

She lifts her head and presses a kiss to my lips. "Me too," she whispers. "It's our forever."

I close my eyes for a moment, drifting into sleep, knowing that this is only the beginning of our forever.

We'll face whatever life throws at us, together. Because together, this life, this family, this home, is exactly what forever was supposed to look like.

I press another soft kiss to Tempany's lips and sigh softly before breaking it with a murmur, "I wouldn't trade a second of it."

She laughs softly, replying with a yawn, "Neither would I. I love you."

For the first time in a long time, I let myself believe it. It was a journey to get here, but it's a forever temptation I'm all in on. "I love you too, Tempany," I tell her, kissing her forward, before pulling back the blankets to cover her. She's already drifting to sleep and murmurs softly, something audible but it doesn't matter anymore. This moment is all that does and every moment until forever.

CHAPTER THIRTY-TWO

Tempany

It's incredible that this day in our lives has finally arrived, years having passed since Ashton asked me to marry him. We've been through so much together and it's made us stronger as a couple.

Today I feel so astoundingly beautiful. My dress is sparkling in the mid morning sun and waiting for Ashton for our first look, I'm thinking about the girls day out hens day party I had with Ava, Dakota, Lorena, Ariel, and some of the girls from work last weekend. The grandparents had the kids for the night and that meant I could really let my hair down. I'd drunk way more than I had in years, having downed way too many cocktails and shots that I lost count. The next day wasn't fun, with my head pounding with the worst hangover I've ever had. Thankfully I'd had the foresight to not plan our wedding for the day after my hens day. Ashton was appreciative of that as well, his bucks night was even more wild. He didn't get home until six am–and he was incoherent–he was that drunk. I didn't get angry, I trust him with my life and even with Zeke being his best mate I know he didn't do anything untoward. He would've told me, and frankly I'd still marry him anyway.

I hear leaves crunching now, his dress shoes crushing them underfoot as he approaches me standing under the willow trees near the beach. They're an icon in Lockgrove Bay, being the only non-native trees in town. When the footsteps recede I turn to face him, smiling so wide I'm afraid I'm going to crack my flawless makeup look.

Ashton grins, standing back to admire my dress. "Wow, Temptress, you look stunning. Your dress is absolutely beautiful. It fits you perfectly."

"Thanks, Simba. Your suit looks dapper."

He takes a step closer to me, embracing me and inhaling my perfume as he kisses my neck. "You smell divine as well, temptress. What perfume is that?"

"Alien," I tell him, smiling when I add, "It's my favourite now, because I know how much you love it."

"It smells delicious on you," he teases with a smirk before kissing me. His kiss is hard, but not forceful and takes my breath away. I'm the luckiest woman in the world to be marrying such an amazing man. He's been great with the twins, and has tried his best to make my life easier by getting up for the early morning feeds before he goes for a run and goes to work.

I know our future together is going to be amazing, our babies will know how much their parents love each other, and be led by example.

Breaking the kiss, Ashton smiles at me, asking, "Ready to go get married, my temptress?"

"Of course I'm ready, my Simba," I reply, beaming as I take his hand and we walk down to the beach together.

Our family and friends are seated on the white chairs set up on the sand, with the arch up the front covered in roses.

At the end of the aisle Ashton drops my hand, walking down the rose petal path to stand under the arch with Zeke and Beau. Ava and Lorena stand from their chairs. They both smile at me before they take turns to walk down the aisle. Ava first and then Lorena. My dad then takes my hand, kissing me on the cheek. "You look stunning, my darling daughter."

"Thank you, dad. I'm so glad to have you by

my side today," I admit, hugging him. "I never thought that would be possible."

"I know, darling," he says, grinning when he adds, "Let's get you married."

Everyone stands, and the music, 'I Am Yours' by *Need to Breathe* starts to play and he leads me down the aisle. I can't believe I'm about to get married. Ashton is beaming, watching me walk towards him, and Zeke elbows him in the side when tears start to fall down his cheeks. He says something to him that I can't make out, but knowing Zeke it's some teasing comment. Their bromance is strong, and knowing that love surrounds us today makes me happy. Nothing could make this moment better.

CHAPTER THIRTY-THREE

Ashton

Tempany stops at the end of the aisle, her dad giving her a kiss on the cheek. The celebrant nods to tell me to step forward and I take her hand so we're standing under the rose arch together. I sniff back the tears, and softly murmur, "You're so beautiful, Tempany."

She has tears in her eyes now, and with my thumb I brush them away to not ruin her flawless makeup. She still looks like herself but even more stunning somehow.

She smiles at me, sniffing back the tears, and I know that smile is just for me. No one else. That smile causes my anxiety to ease, for the knot in my chest to loosen so I'm breathing normally again. My heart is still racing, but in a good way. I'm about to marry my temptress, the love of my life.

Still clutching her hands in mine, I sigh and focus on only her until everything else fades away and it's just us at this moment. All I see is her. The woman who knows me, fully, who's loved me since we were kids just shooting hoops on the basketball court. The woman who despite our hardships has been by my side through it all.

The celebrant starts the ceremony. I'm not really paying attention, not properly anyway. The words are a blur, jumbled mumblings that mean nothing. I just want to get to the good part. To the announcement that Tempany is mine forever, that she is my wife. Her fingers grip mine tighter, grounding me and reminding me that this is us, we're here together.

When it's time for our vows, I swallow hard. I'd prepared vows, but in the moment, even though I'd rehearsed them over and over in my mind I can't think of them. Instead, I look into her eyes and begin, "Tempany, you came back into my life without warning. You didn't push, just let our love grow and changed my whole life for the better."

Her lower lip trembles, as though she's fighting back more tears. I want to kiss her, but it's not time yet.

"You see all of me, the real Ashton. The real one that I can't hide from when things can be hard. And instead of walking away, you chose to stand right here with me and exchange vows with me, to say '*I love you, Simba.*'"

She's about to respond but I swallow hard, cutting her off and continuing, "I can't promise a life filled with perfection, because we both know that's not possible. But I promise I'll keep choosing you, loving you—even on the days when it's hard. Honestly, especially on those days, because that's when our love is strongest."

She nods, her tears breaking free now.

"Ashton, my love, my Simba, I choose you," she says softly as she squeezes my hand still in hers. "I will choose you every day, forever. I want to be your temptress, forever and love you for all of my days."

Her words are simple. They're not overwhelming promises, of this and that. Just a promise that we'll be together forever, that she will be my forever temptation.

The celebrant pauses, and Zeke hands me the rings, which we slip onto each other's fingers. It's a shared moment where nothing else matters, but Tempany and I connecting ourselves together.

I hear the words of the celebrant, the traditional announcement, "You may now kiss the bride."

I don't hesitate, leaning in to kiss her like I've

been waiting my whole life to do it right here, right now. Like this moment belongs to us, the beginning of our forever.

Applause erupts around us, with a few hollers and whoops, which I'm sure is Zeke and Beau being their usual selves. I can hear someone crying, which is most likely my mum. But I'm confident that would be happy tears. She probably never thought I'd get married.

I rest my forehead against Tem's. "We're married, finally, temptress," I murmur.

She smiles, and she's utterly radiant. "Yeah," she whispers, "We are." I take her hand again, turning to face our family and friends. We walk toward them, ready for our forever that I'm finally ready for.

CHAPTER THIRTY-FOUR
Ezekiel

The babies are coming–soon–so I'm knee deep in dad tasks, folding the baby clothes Ava has washed and putting them in the drawers. Each kid has their own set of drawers, each with matching sets of clothes in gender neutral colours since we didn't find out what we're having. In between I'm pacing the room in total panic mode to distract myself whilst I wait for a call from the hospital.

Ava has been in the hospital for over a week now, on bedrest and around the clock monitoring due to the risk of her having preeclampsia. Of course that has me on edge, with my phone attached to my hip. My phone rings just as I'm closing the drawer after putting in the last onesie with an unknown number. My breath hitches, and for a second, I don't answer. I don't want to answer. But know I have to.

At the last second, I slide my finger over the screen to answer and the voice I hear isn't the hospital.

"I'm coming home, little dufus," the voice says.

I stay silent, the disbelief hitting me hard in the chest whilst I inhale a deep breath. Questions tumble out. "When? Why now?"

Dane exhales, his breathing becoming shallower. "I was injured in action."

"Oh shit, D. Are you ok?"

"Not really, but I get to come home."

"When?" I repeat, gulping down the lump in my throat. I honestly don't think I can deal with Dane coming home right now, with the birth of the twins about to happen any day now. I know he's going to be a different person. War changes people, and Dane has been through a lot more than he's been privy to share.

"Soon, little dufus. Soon."

I don't even have a moment to process with another call incoming.

"D, I gotta go," I mumble, hanging up on my brother to answer the other call without waiting for his response.

"Hello Ezekiel, this is Loralee from the hospital calling to tell you that Ava has gone into active labour."

"Oh um, yep, ok," I stammer, sensing the urgency in her voice.

"It would be best for you to make your way to the hospital as soon as possible."

"Ok, thank you," I respond, my voice shaking as I hang up.

In haste I grab my keys from the kitchen table. They hit the floor the second I grab them. I curse myself, under my breath, crouching down to grab them. They slip through my fingers and I have to mentally tell myself to slow down. Take a deep breath.

Once out on the road, the drive is a blur. My mind is full of incomplete thoughts. Twins. Hospital. Dane. Home. At every stop I'm gripping the steering for dear life, wordlessly urging the lights to change. My jaw is clenched so tight it aches.

With the traffic being so busy–and in my altered mental state–I miss the turn into the car park and have to do an illegal u-turn. My clenched fingers are white on the steering wheel. *Pull yourself together, man*, I chastise myself. Ava needs me present.

Once inside the hospital it feels as though everything is on fast mode. I'm already so overwhelmed and all I can see is doors. All I can hear are voices. I rush to Ava's room, my body running on muscle memory alone. My phone buzzes in my pocket again—Dane, probably calling back because I hung up on him—but I can't bring myself to look at it, let alone answer right now.

My mind won't slow down. What if I'm too late. What if I forgot something. What if I fail her.

Reaching her room I realise my hands are shaking and clammy. I wipe them on my jeans and try to ground myself before I enter the room.

Now I'm at the hospital my thoughts still won't settle.

Dane is coming home.

Ava is in labour.

I can't help but think of what if's. Mainly what if something goes wrong?

I don't let myself finish that thought. I know better than that. Know that it's just fear talking.

I'm here for Ava. To witness the birth of our children.

Ava is just behind the closed door, and the only thing I can control here is how I react once I step into that room. I just want everything to go well, for my babies to be healthy and my girl to be safe. But with her body already out to harm her I'm terrified of losing her. That's what is getting to me the most. The thought of gaining something precious, but losing her.

When I finally open the door and enter the room, Ava looks beautiful. It's clear to see she's exhausted but she's unbreakable. Her eyes are sharp with focus. Walking over to the bed, I grip her hand and she squeezes it hard enough to hurt when a contraction hits her. I welcome the pain. It means our babies are coming. It means it's time. I glance at the midwife, and then back to Ava when I tell her, "You're doing so good, firefly." It's not words to reassure her, it's just stating a fact.

Time blurs then, the midwife encouraging Ava to push through. I just hold her hand, grimacing through the pain when she squeezes it so tightly I'm afraid she'll break it. It's nothing on the pain she's experiencing.

Without warning there's a cry, a loud wail of a cry—and then the world stops completely with the midwife announcing, "It's a girl."

I look at Ava, and she murmurs, "Zaylah." We'd decided on a couple names for each gender. But Ava had loved the name Zaylah from the moment we'd seen it on the baby names website.

Zaylah is unbelievably tiny. Her face is red, and her cries show outrage towards the world she's just arrived in. Just looking at her steals the air from my lungs. I'm barely able to take her in before baby two is making an entrance, with a softer wail. This time it's a boy. My very own mini me like Zaylah will be Ava's.

"Elias," Ava mumbles.

I focus on my babies then. Not the constant beeping from the monitors, not even Ava's breathing. I focus on my heart hammering as the fear I've been holding in finally breaks free.

Awe.

Relief.

Love.

They're here. My babies are here. A boy and a girl. Elias and Zaylah.

My world didn't implode.

The midwife lays the babies on Ava's chest, one on each side.

Ava looks ruined and radiant at the same time. She smiles at our babies, and then meets my eyes over their heads. In that moment there's no fear left—it's just us, our love, and what we made together.

I admire my babies, saying, "They're perfect, firefly. You did so well."

My thoughts turn back to my brother coming home. I don't want the distance anymore. I just want my brother. I'm glad he's coming home, but I'm also terrified he's going to be a completely different person.

I pick up Elias, cradling him in my arms whilst

Ava holds Zaylah. We both ground ourselves in that moment, not wanting to shatter the newborn bubble by not being present. My phone buzzes in my pocket. Carefully I yank it out, awkwardly because of the precious cargo in my arms. I glance at it and feel my tension melt away a little.

On my way. Landing soon.

The worry is still there. But I can only hope for the best.

Looking down at my newborn son in my arms I understand, finally, that I don't need to worry about what life throws at me. I can handle it. I just need to have hope.

Epilogue

ASHTON

ABOUT ONE YEAR LATER

Christmas morning at the Castello house starts before I'm even ready to open my damn eyes. Our kids had stumbled out of bed, bleary eyed but excited for opening presents just as the sun was rising.

Zeke, Ava, Dane, and the kids had stayed overnight with us, and we'd all gone to bed too late for Christmas Eve, not to mention us boys had drunk way too much to be functioning so early in the morning.

Tempany and I head into the lounge room to find the twins sitting by the Christmas tree, their eyes boggling at the presents stacked there. I watch Tempany go over and give each of them a present to open. Within mere seconds there's paper everywhere—torn, crumpled, and discarded to get into the good stuff inside.

Ander is first, opening his zoo Duplo and he lets out a giddy scream, holding it up to me. "Daddy, Duplo zoo," he says, smiling wide.

"Yeah, buddy, you're going to have a great time building that."

Ander is obsessed with animals of every kind, but especially furry ones like big cats and foxes, and strangely also dingoes. He thinks they're actually dogs. I don't tell him they're not, and I'd thought about getting the family a dog—a Belgian Malinos to be specific—for Christmas, but Tempany and I both decided the twins are too young yet for a dog. Aliah opens her first present then—a baby alive doll—and her shriek of excitement is so loud it fills the room and bounces off the walls.

"Dolly, Dolly!" she screams out. Tempany elbows me in the side, nodding down at our daughter and sniggering as we watch her tear at the box to get the doll out like a possessed animal.

It's chaos already. Tempany bends down to help her and I turn towards the hallway, watching as Zeke and Ava stumble in, holding their twins, one on each hip.

"Morning, Merry Christmas," I greet them, nodding.

Zeke mumbles his reply, rubbing the sleep from his eyes, "Merry Christmas, bro."

Ava puts Zaylah down on the floor next to Aliah, and glances at the presents before picking one up and showing her daughter. She smiles, even though she has no idea what is going on. Zeke puts Elias down, and Tempany fusses over him as I head to the kitchen with Zeke following me.

"Coffee, bro?" I ask, powering on the coffee machine.

"Fuck, yeah. My head is screaming at me right now."

"You and me both, bro. The kids have already been shrieking like banshees."

Reaching up, I grab out two large mugs out of the cupboard. Zeke grabs the milk frother jug out of the fridge, handing it to me to connect it to the coffee machine. Thankfully it's quick and in minutes we're both clutching mugs of coffee as though they're a lifeline. This coffee is so dark roasted—and not bitter—that it could wake up a patient from a coma. It's the real deal, and Zeke clearly needs it right now. His eyes are bloodshot, and he's completely spaced out as he sips his coffee, leaning against the counter. Mine probably look worse. I barely slept a wink last night.

We don't speak. It's not time for words, when a look towards the lounge room says it all—*we're all exhausted, we're on the verge of being outnumbered —as more family and friends will be arriving after breakfast, if we even get to eating anything—but this is exactly where we're meant to be. This is the life we want and love, despite all the hardships.*

A shrill shriek cuts through the room as one of the twins protests having help with opening their present. I honestly don't know if it was one of mine or theirs, but Ava's there instantly, calming Elias, lifting him against her chest. She's a great mum. She looks tired, but settled and happy. Grounded. Just watching our kids with their mothers makes everything else fade into the background.

After the kids have opened all their presents, Tempany comes wandering into the kitchen, giving me a smile.

"I guess we should get to making some breakfast," she verbalises with a sigh. I feel that in my bones. Just the thought of making breakfast for everyone seems like way too much effort.

"What did you have in mind?" I ask, hoping she's not going to ask me to whip up bacon and eggs. I'm way too tired to even contemplate that task.

"Maybe pancakes. There's a couple pancake shakers in the pantry."

"On it," I reply, skidding across the kitchen to the pantry. The pancake shakers are right in front of me, two exactly. Taking them out, I shake them and dance around the kitchen. Zeke eyes me, laughing.

"You right there, Ash? Something odd in your coffee that wasn't in mine?"

"Nope," I sing-song, "Just trying to wake myself up and have a bit of fun. It's Christmas after all."

"Fair enough, bro. Anything I can help with?"

As I start to pour water into the bottles, I reply, "Do you mind checking if anyone else wants a coffee or tea?"

"Sure thing," Zeke responds, heading back into the lounge room to see if Dane is awake. I'd be surprised if he's not, seeing as he was sleeping on the couch. The chaos in the lounge room around the Christmas tree was loud enough to wake the dead. As quickly as I can, I busy myself making the pancakes–dreading the arrival of my family and the rest of her friends in mere hours. But at the same time I'm excited for this to be the first of many Christmases in our household.

TEMPANY

I'm already beyond exhausted. We've eaten too many pancakes and I'm busily rushing around the kitchen, getting the roast chicken, beef, and ham into the oven for lunch. Our parents, Dakota and Knox with Aspen, and Lorena and Beau with Grady and Lucy, as well as Piper, will be arriving before lunch. They're all bringing a vegetable dish—or two—and Piper is arriving later and didn't stay overnight like Dane did because she's at the bakery getting dessert finalised. She was super secretive about it, but said it was going to be mindblowing and a new Christmas favourite.

Speaking of Dane, he's sprawled on the couch, one arm hooked around Elias—his nephew who is besotted with him—the other is balancing his mug of coffee that still has a sip in the bottom. I'm surprised he hasn't spilled yet. He's still a bit out of it, but the boys had a night of drinking and Dane struggles more than most with that these days. He's definitely improved since being home, and since Piper is in his life. I know things aren't serious with them yet, but I don't doubt it will happen. They're sweet together. They ground each other.

Everyone is in the lounge room now, gathered

around the Christmas tree, sitting on either the couches or the floor.

Out of the blue, like he's asking about the weather, Dane says, "So when's the wedding, Ezekiel?"

The room stills. I swear I can hear Zeke gulp.

From the kitchen I see Ava stiffen, and her eyes sink. She wants to say something, but Dane didn't direct the question to her. Zeke groans, dragging a hand down his face, half-smiling like he's been ambushed.

"Do we have to bring this up before lunch?" he asks.

"Yes," Ashton responds immediately, his voice teasing. Laughter ripples through the room, but everyone is invested, staring Zeke down, waiting for his answer. Ava is the most invested. It's almost as though she's about to break, and scream out something obscene.

Zeke exhales, mumbling, "I want to wait for a bit longer."

Ava glares at him, and huffs.

"Not because I'm unsure," he adds quickly. "I'm not. I just... I want the twins to be a bit older."

Silence falls on the room, only gasps escaping some of us.

"I want them to be part of the day," he says, voice even. Certain. "I want them to be present and to have more of an idea of what is happening."

I get it, I understand his reasoning. It's not that he doesn't want to marry Ava. He just wants his family to be a part of their forever.

Ava huffs again. "That's ages away, Zeke!" Her eye roll is dramatic enough to draw a few grins from around the room.

"I want it to be our special day," she says. "The celebration where I get to wear the white dress and to declare our love in front of our family and friends."

Zeke doesn't argue. He nods, meeting her gaze. His gaze is steady and unapologetic, like he's already accepted his fate. He's getting married sooner rather than later, and waiting until the twins are walking may not be an option if Ava gets her way.

"You see my point though, Av's?" he asks, his voice raspy and a little unsteady.

She exhales slowly. "Fine," she huffs. "But I'm picking the date."

The tension shifts, everyone breaking down into laughter. Zeke leans over to kiss her forehead, grinning like he knows he's won the lottery.

THE DAY MOVES ON QUICKLY AFTER THAT, A blur with our guests arriving and lunch being served and stretching longer than planned. The kids run around, hyped on sugar and loud. The babies are passed back and forth between mothers and grandmothers.

I watch Zeke and Ava together—not from the outside, not like I'm witnessing something separate from my own life—but from inside the same moment. We're all learning how to wait these days. Not because life is paused, but because it's full.

We're all together, living our lives, our forever's which are full, of kindy mornings and then school shoes by the door. Of Christmases together just like this one. And of weddings, of our family expanding with more love.

Nothing could be better.

By evening, after all of our guests have gone, the house settles into a softer kind of noise. My twins are half asleep on the couch, their limbs tangled together and their cheeks flushed from exhaustion. I gather them up on my hip, taking them to their cots.

Giving them both a kiss on the forehead, I stand back and let my mind wander back over the day, over the year—the mess, the laughter, the chaos and the calm. This is my life. A life we've built together, from the very beginning. It's a life filled with love and the promise of forever.

The forever we grew into.

What's next for Lockgrove Bay?

If you're like me you never want to leave Lockgrove Bay. If you haven't read the *Bay Hearts* Trilogy (mmf/mm) then go grab those to catch up with some of these characters, and whilst you're getting them grab *The Dreams* duet (mm) to meet some more of the parents and kids, because we're not leaving Lockgrove Bay yet.

There's one more book after this in the parents' stories, which is Dane Alessio's story. And that will be full of heartbreak and steamy moments with a beautiful happily ever after.

Then it's the kids stories beginning with the *Bay Kisses* series which will be eight books long (at the moment) and is a mix of mf and mm stories, all with some type of forbidden trope. There is also a prequel to *Bay Kisses* called *All Over You* which introduces you to some of the kids grown up.

The first book *(Stolen Kisses)* is a foster/step-brother mm romance between Peyton Sullivan & Grayson Barnes with some dark themes, bi-awakening x2, and a whole lot of angst, drama, and spicy times in true Caz style. (Parents are Aidan and Thayer from *In Your Dreams-Dreams* duet #1)

Acknowledgments

Again we come to end of another book, and I don't really know where to begin with this.

Honestly I need to thank my readers of this series. The love for Ashton and Tempany is what prompted me to write a second book about them, continuing their happy ever after.

It's been a long time coming with this story, and sometimes I never thought I'd ever get this story finished. But it's here, and I'm glad to be back sharing stories with you all.

I need to thank my amazing editor Samantha Wolf. She read and edited this story multiple times to help make it the best it can be. And without her, it would be a big mess of mixed up timelines and craziness.

I'd also like to thank my amazing partner, Nathan. He is beyond supportive of my writing and is always encouraging me to continue with my passion for writing words.

Also by Caz May

All available on Amazon. Some titles are in Kindle Unlimited.

Lockgrove Bay Series

(Reading order as listed)

Be Tempted Duet

Bk 1-Loathing Temptation

Bk 2 Wicked Temptation

Bay Hearts Trilogy

Bk 1 Wild Hearts

Bk 2 Tamed Hearts

Bk 3 Unbreakable

(best read after Take my Heart)

My Heart Duet

Bk 1-Take My Heart

Dreams Duet

(best read after the Bay Hearts Trilogy with or without the others or as a standalone duet)

Bk 1 In Your Dreams

Bk 2 In My Dreams

Heart Voyager Duet

Bk 1 Let Time Be

My Girl Duet

Bk 1-Not my Girl

Bk 2-Still my Girl

Always Only You Series

Bk 1-Roommates Don't Kiss & Tell

Bk 2-Friends Don't Say Goodbye

Bk 3-Feelings Don't Play Fair

Bk 4-Hearts Don't Steer Us Wrong

The Mackenney Family Saga

Bk 1-Country Secrets

Bk 2-Doctor Attraction

Bk 3-Unlawful Attachment

A Holiday Romance Duet

(Can be read as standalones)

Bk 1-Take Flight

Bk 2-Secret Santa

Jingle Balls

Words of Love & Life (Poetry)

About the Author

Caz May is a librarian/teacher by trade but was always destined to be an author from a young age. In her spare time, she can be found devouring books or writing her own stories with characters that may not be the typical romance heroes but are loveable just as much.
She lives for Iced coffee, but pretty much just loves food in general.
When she's not writing or reading a book most likely she can probably be found asleep, reading or binge-watching the latest show or movie.
Check out her Instagram or other socials to get in touch. Please don't forget to review on Goodreads and Amazon.

Sign up for my newsletter, or check out my website
www.cazmayauthor.com
to get news on all things Caz May.

facebook.com/CazMayAuthor

instagram.com/cazmayauthor

amazon.com/Caz-May/e/B088P6BF1W

bookbub.com/profile/caz-may

goodreads.com/cazmay

pinterest.com/cazmayauthor

tiktok.com/@cazmayauthor